The Col

Auc
Published by Audrey Harrison

Find more about the author and contact details at the end of this book and the chance to obtain a free copy of The Unwilling Earl.
Proofread and edited by Joan O'Kelley
Oh1kelley@gmail.com
Cover by Historical Editorial
http://www.historicalfictionbookcovers.com/

Prologue

Netherfield, Hertfordshire, 1813

With his ready smile on his face, Colonel Richard Fitzwilliam entered the bedchamber of his cousin. Darcy frowned at him, at which Fitzwilliam's smile broadened.

"The nerves getting to you?" he asked, as Darcy's valet fussed around his cousin.

"Why am I so nervous? I want this wedding to take place, but my stomach is behaving like I'm some sort of callow youth on his first adventure," Darcy said, with a nod dismissing his valet. He looked resplendent in a blue frock coat and cream breeches; his boots had been polished until they shone in the sunlight.

"It is good to be nervous," Fitzwilliam reassured his relation. "But I'm convinced they are unnecessary doubts."

Darcy finished fiddling with his neckcloth. He normally spent an age perfecting the gentle folds, but today he was even more inclined than usual for it to look impeccable. "I know you speak the truth. But it does not help that I'd rather not be the centre of attention for the morning."

"I have some bad news to break to you, Darcy. No one is interested in you. They all want to see your bride in her wedding dress. All the women will be wondering if there will be lace or if she will wear flowers in her hair or a bonnet, or even a feather! You, my friend, are so low down in everyone's interest, you are virtually not needed to attend," Fitzwilliam said.

Darcy laughed. Those who did not know him well, would wonder at the uncommon occurrence, but to the few people who were dear to him, it was a regular, natural sound. "Good! Thank you, Fitzwilliam. I needed to be brought to the reality of the day. I too often allow myself to overthink a simple situation."

"You? My dear cousin, I don't know what you could possibly mean!"

Darcy shook his head at his cousin but then became serious. "Fitzwilliam, can I ask you a question in which I need your reply to be very honest?"

"Sounds ominous."

"It is something I should have raised before now. I know I'm a blockhead for needing to ask, but the niggle will not go away. You and Elizabeth — at Rosings, you were…"

Fitzwilliam looked at his cousin with sympathy. He was a man with ten thousand pounds a year, a capable landlord of one of the largest estates in Derbyshire, and yet he could be so unsure of himself. It endeared him further with the cousin who, in many ways, was more like a brother.

"Darcy, I promise you this. I was never in love with Elizabeth, nor she, me. I admit, I think her handsome, funny, and one of the best people I will soon have the pleasure to call cousin, but there are no other feelings towards her. And never have been," Fitzwilliam said honestly.

"I can see why she would be drawn to you," Darcy said, still looking uncomfortable.

Moving over to put his hands on his cousin's shoulders, Fitzwilliam shook him gently. "She turned your first proposal down because she did not truly know you at that time. Plus the fact that the blackguard, Wickham, had

4

been whispering poison into her ear and the general of her town."

It had been a hard time for Darcy, blundering in and causing what had appeared to be a permanent breach with the woman he'd asked to marry him. He had only confessed the whole situation afterwards to his cousin, after he'd actually secured Elizabeth's affection.

"I could understand if there had been an attraction..."

"No! There was mild flirtation. You know my character and hers. Neither of us can resist being playful, but she is yours Darcy. I am certain she always was. Your good opinion mattered too much to her to be disinterested. Look how she was with the buffoon, Collins — civil but cool. She was never that with you. From the start, there was something between you. Call it a spark if you like. But you were drawn to each other and teased and tormented one another from the beginning. That evening in Rosings in which she played the pianoforte was a prime example. She was far more playful towards you than at any other time with anyone else. We had been speaking. When you arrived, she started to tease you. Trust me on this. You have always been the only man for her."

Darcy sighed. "Thank you. Again. It's just the emotions of today. I am doubting everything that is poor in my character and all that I have known. I feel very unsure, and it is causing me some strange thoughts. I will relax. I will."

"Good. This uncertainty does you no credit, especially towards Elizabeth. You should be convinced of her regard. We can all see it. She is besotted with you and rightly so. It is time, for once, that you relax and enjoy yourself, Darcy. You deserve happiness," Fitzwilliam pointed out. "And, you know me. I won't look at any young woman with serious consideration unless she has at least five thousand a year and three properties, one in London, a hunting lodge in Leicester, and a grand mansion in the country, preferably somewhere near Derbyshire."

"You tell a good Banbury tale, cousin. You would never be so shallow."

"I'm the second son. I cannot afford to be anything but particular about what a wife brings to the marriage. Otherwise, we will starve."

Smiling, Darcy picked up his stove top and placed it on his head. "Come. Let's go and get this over with. The sooner I make Elizabeth Mrs. Darcy, the better."

"That's the spirit," Fitzwilliam laughed, but inside he felt a little jealous of his cousin. Oh, he had spoken the truth when he confessed that he'd never had feelings for Elizabeth. He had enjoyed her company but hadn't been anywhere near falling in love with her. He was envious of a couple so perfectly suited setting out on their future life together.

They would have hurdles to overcome, mainly because of the family on both sides, but they were a strong couple who would support and love each other. Fitzwilliam was sure and was glad of it. Darcy had lost his father and mother when he was young and yet had to be brother and parent to his younger sister. He had taken on the role without complaint, but it was now time for him to have his own family.

Fitzwilliam longed to have that connection with someone, but his pocket and birth dictated that he was forced to look for a wife who brought a comfortable dowry to the marriage. His income as a colonel barely covered the costs of his uniform and the horseflesh he needed. His allowance from his father made sure his officer's mess bill was paid each quarter with a little left over, but without the occasional monetary gifts from his Aunt Catherine and Darcy, he would struggle to keep out of dun territory. That was not conducive when hoping to set-up home or start a family.

Yet those were the two things he longed for.

Chapter 1

London – three years later, late summer 1816

Fitzwilliam walked into the Darcy house on Berkeley Square, striding through the familiar property where he had stayed so often over the years. The last few years had aged him. War did that to a person. Oh, he was still a gentleman whose personality was all ease and pleasing, but there were a few frown lines permanently set in his features and a more serious set to his expression when he thought he was unobserved.

He had not seen his cousin and his cousin's wife for months and was looking forward to an evening full of good company and family chat, something he had missed over the last few years.

He walked unannounced into the drawing room, and Elizabeth immediately stood to greet him.

"Colonel Fitzwilliam! You have arrived at last! How lovely it is to see you. It has been too long," Elizabeth said, holding out her hands in welcome.

"It has indeed," Fitzwilliam responded. "You are looking extremely well, Cousin."

Elizabeth blushed slightly. "Thank you. There are only three months to wait, and then there will be yet another Darcy polluting the grounds of Pemberley." She smiled at the reference her connection to the family had stirred from Lady Catherine De Bourgh when she had first become aware of her nephew's affection for Elizabeth.

Lady Catherine was the formidable aunt to Darcy and Fitzwilliam on their mothers' side of the family and never restrained herself from making her observations known to those around her.

"That will make us a family of four, and I want there to be at least a dozen, so the grounds of Pemberley are doomed," Darcy said with a grin at his wife whilst approaching his cousin. "Fitzwilliam, I have missed you. Little Richard has barely seen his namesake," Darcy said of his firstborn.

"And I've missed you," Fitzwilliam admitted. He'd spent the last year in France, fighting against Napoleon's troops until their defeat at Waterloo and then had remained abroad overseeing some of the rebuilding of relationships between the two formerly warring countries. He'd already fought in the Peninsular Wars in Spain and was battle weary and had been homesick for some time. "Hopefully with Napoleon's abdication, there will be peace in Europe once more, but this time, of the long-lasting kind."

"It is time for you to enjoy some entertainments," Elizabeth said. "And to have some sustaining food. You have lost weight since we saw you last."

"There wasn't enough food to feed two warring armies. Then there was a poor harvest, so they are still struggling," Fitzwilliam said of the hardships they'd suffered. He didn't want to dwell on his time abroad, so he quickly changed the subject. "Unfortunately, there will be no joviality around town for me. Our aunt's letter and Darcy's need to get you to Pemberley in good time for the arrival of the baby means I shall be heading to Rosings for the foreseeable future," Fitzwilliam said. "I do think it's unkind of you to abandon me to a trip to Rosings alone."

Darcy smiled. They'd always gone together on trips to their aunt. Lady Catherine De Bourgh was a force indeed, and her instructions, opinions, and directions were always given expecting no argument. That Darcy very often did meant Fitzwilliam was needed to smooth the waters between the pair. Lady Catherine had been determined that Darcy would marry her only daughter, a sickly creature who always looked terrified in Darcy's presence, but that had been of no concern to her mother. Darcy's falling in love with Elizabeth had brought the wrath of Lady Catherine on both Darcy and Elizabeth as never before, and as a result, there was a breach between them that had not been completely healed.

"As you are her favourite nephew, it is your task to try to glean what has been happening at Rosings. She would have a spasm if she saw Elizabeth increasing for a second time," Darcy said.

"Spasm indeed! That woman has never had a day's illness in her life! Although, I admit she wouldn't be a doting great aunt," Fitzwilliam said. "I must confess, I had to sit down when I read her letter. Had you any idea of our secret relatives?"

Darcy shook his head. "No. Absolutely nothing. Another aunt. I was always told that there were three sisters: your mother, mine, and Aunt Catherine. How could we have not known that there was a fourth?"

"It did make me chuckle to read her words, 'I thought while we had to accept the Bennet family into our midst, it was time to invite our youngest sister's child into the family. She has been motherless these last ten years and has the misfortune to have a cotton worker as a father. My own dear father, quite rightly, forbad the match, but there was a dash to the border, and the deed was done. She was cast off from that day to the grime of Manchester and wasn't allowed into the family crypt when she died.' The poor woman had a lucky escape. Could you imagine being forced to lie beside Aunt Catherine for eternity when she eventually passes? Please do not inflict that fate on me, Darcy," Fitzwilliam appealed.

"You are a cad," Darcy said in answer to the request.

"I am being perfectly serious."

"What else does she write about your cousin? Is it not an odd thing to do, to invite her to Rosings? She clearly has no affection for the girl," Elizabeth said, not wishing the strained atmosphere of that house on anyone, least of all a girl who must be completely out of her social circle.

"She goes on to mention that Mrs. Jenkinson, Cousin Anne's companion, has hurt her back and has been shipped off to her sister's home for the foreseeable future. I think a free substitute for Mrs. Jenkinson was our aunt's motivation rather than any benevolent feelings towards this unknown cousin of ours," Fitzwilliam explained.

"Ah, I now understand completely," Elizabeth said with a smile. "The poor girl. I do not envy her position or the welcome she will receive. I wonder if she realises she is to be companion to Anne," Elizabeth said of Lady Catherine's only daughter.

"Exactly my sentiments. Which is why I have to fall on my sword and attend Rosings without the support of Darcy," Fitzwilliam said. "She is five and twenty, apparently an only child, and her father still works in Manchester."

"Strange that he should agree to allow her to come for a visit after all this time. He must know what Aunt Catherine is like, to some extent at least," Darcy said.

"Although if she isn't wed, perhaps he is looking for her to become a companion and feels she could benefit with learning what the role entails. Better than working in a mill for the rest of her life."

"It's all very intriguing," Elizabeth said. "I almost wish I could accompany you. But not quite."

Fitzwilliam laughed. "I'd appreciate the help from either of you. Aunt Catherine is going to be in top form. It would probably take the three of us to protect the poor girl. I wonder: Does she know what she has let herself in for?"

"She might have already run back to Manchester by the time you get there," Elizabeth said.

"That is presuming she can afford the coach fare, for you can guarantee, however rough and uncivilised she is, Aunt Catherine won't give up the opportunity for free services easily," Darcy warned. "I shall look forward to your letters."

"And I shall look forward to Charlotte's," Elizabeth said with reference to her best friend, who was the wife of Elizabeth's cousin, the clergyman attached to Rosings. Although Charlotte had married a man who was lacking in sensibility, she remained a dear friend to Elizabeth and had travelled to spend some time with Elizabeth at Pemberley. That this had occurred at one of the busiest times of the year for any clergyman had not been a coincidence. Inflicting the prosaic personality of Mr. Collins on her husband was not something Elizabeth was prepared to do.

"Anyway, enough of our family's deep dark secrets. Tell us more of your travels. I am glad you returned to us safely," Darcy said of his cousin.

"As am I, Darcy. As am I."

*

Fitzwilliam rode horseback to Rosings rather than take his carriage. He was a man used to being outdoors, and days spent confined in a vehicle did not appeal to him. He would be restricted enough when he arrived at his destination, because Lady Catherine De Bourgh demanded constant attention from her guests. Which was another of the many reasons he had always visited with Darcy.

Turning onto the estate of Rosings, Fitzwilliam felt his shoulders set even though he was still in the saddle. The grandeur of the building, the opulence of the interior, and the whole self-importance of the place and its residents were such as to give a constant air of aloofness. It was a formal, unwelcoming place.

It was going to be a long few weeks.

After he entered the large hallway, one of the many servants employed by his aunt relieved him of his greatcoat. He idly wondered if any but the ones in close contact with his aunt actually worked very hard. There always seemed to be an abundance of staff, far too many for the family who resided there.

He was informed that Lady Catherine was resting in her chamber, but that Miss Anne was in the drawing room with Miss Bamber. Presuming this was the name of his newly found cousin, he entered the room. Fitzwilliam faltered slightly before continuing into the large square space. He had never seen Anne look so well.

Immediately recollecting himself, he approached his cousin, bowing over her outstretched hand. "Cousin Anne, you are looking particularly fine this morning. It is a pleasure to see you," he said. It was true. Anne had colour in her cheeks. She was a small, thin girl, prone to a pinched expression and feebleness. When he'd walked in, she had been laughing with her companion, cheeks rosy and eyes shining — something Fitzwilliam had never seen before. It had warmed his insides to see such a difference in his cousin.

Anne blushed. "I have started to ride out with Prudence every morning in a gig. We do it before my mother comes below stairs. She wouldn't be happy at my spending so much time out of doors, but I feel the benefit of it."

Fitzwilliam was staggered by two things: first, that his cousin was daring to go against her mother, and second, that she'd uttered more than one sentence at a time. Suddenly, his stay had become far more interesting.

He turned to Prudence. "And you must be my secret cousin," he said with an engaging smile. "Richard Fitzwilliam, colonel of the finest dragoons at your service ma'am." Bowing with a flourish, Fitzwilliam grinned at Prudence. He might not be the most handsome man one would ever see, his features being plain rather than striking, but he certainly had address and was always extremely personable. Green eyes laughed out of a face more rounded than the typically sharp aristocratic face, but his wide smile was very appealing.

Prudence stood and offered her hand in greeting. "Prudence Bamber. Pleased to meet you. So, you're the famous colonel. Anne has been telling me all about my relations since my arrival." She was a young woman, tall and slender, one who would be classed as striking rather than pretty. She had angular features, but laughing grey eyes and a ready smile softened her appearance. Her looks reminded Fitzwilliam of his Aunt Darcy, who had been considered extremely attractive in her youth.

"Unfortunately, I'm only famous in the very small circle that consists of my family, outside of which, I am just another military man," Fitzwilliam said pleasantly. He couldn't help but be amused at Prudence's northern accent. His aunt probably wouldn't introduce her as a relation on the grounds of that alone. "I hope you are settling into life at Rosings."

"It's not like any house I have ever stayed in before," Prudence admitted.

"No. Nor I," Fitzwilliam responded with a twinkle in his eye. In his eyes, her comment wasn't a sign that she hadn't been used to the higher echelons of society in claiming she'd never seen such a place. Most people would be surprised and a little over-awed at the excessive opulence displayed in every room at Rosings. Lady Catherine believed in making visitors fully aware of the wealth and status of the family who owned the house. "I'm very interested in your story. I must say neither myself nor our cousin Darcy had any inkling about you."

"No. We are the side of the family best forgotten," Prudence said, sitting down. Her tone was not recriminatory in any way. "It is nice to meet you. I've heard a lot about you and your — sorry — our cousin Darcy. It is taking a little getting used to, knowing that I have cousins."

"But you've not heard about his wife, Elizabeth?" Fitzwilliam asked.

"Oh, yes. A little." Prudence smiled.

"I thought it would be odd for Aunt Catherine not to have informed you how the whole family is going to the dogs."

"Mother is becoming more accustomed to the marriage," Anne said in defence of her parent. "In fact she intends to write with suggestions and recommendations for when the new baby arrives. She did with their first born, and she wishes to ensure Cousin Elizabeth is under no doubt what to do."

"That is good of her. I'm sure Elizabeth will appreciate the correspondence," Fitzwilliam responded, noting Prudence's bland expression at Anne's words and appreciating it. "Now, tell me. What entertainments have you got planned whilst I'm here?"

Anne smiled. "You know we do little entertaining and even less exploring. You could take Prudence and show her beyond the boundary wall. I've never dared to. It would be bad enough if Mother found out about our morning rides. Even worse if we were seen outside the grounds."

"But you do go outside," Fitzwilliam said.

"Yes. But only when mother has arranged everything."

"Ah, I see."

"Is that my nephew? Why was I not told immediately of his arrival?" echoed the voice of the lady of the house as she entered the room.

Anne immediately withdrew into herself, seeming to grow smaller even though she hadn't actually moved. Her look was that of a wary, frightened sparrow. She had lost the colour from her flushed cheeks.

Fitzwilliam had wondered at his aunt not noticing the positive change in Anne, but when he saw the result of Lady Catherine's entrance on her daughter, he completely understood how the two women were able to keep their excursions secret. He felt real sympathy for the effect his aunt had on his young cousin.

"Richard, at last we see you! Arrived safe and sound. Are the family well?"

"They are, indeed, ma'am," Fitzwilliam said, standing and kissing his aunt's proffered cheek. "Mother and everyone else send their best wishes."

"Yes. Yes. Sit yourself down and tell me all your news. Prudence, make yourself useful and ring for a tray to be brought."

"Yes, Aunt," Prudence said, standing and moving to the fireplace to tug on the rope at the side of the marble surround.

"I could have done that," Fitzwilliam said. "Especially as I'm still upright."

"You can come and sit near me and tell me the latest on dits."

Fitzwilliam dutifully obeyed and spent the next half hour pandering to his aunt's questions. When the tea tray was brought into the room, Prudence dutifully poured the tea and then handed around the cups. When the cups were emptied, she collected them and rang for the tray to be removed, reinforcing Fitzwilliam's assumption that she was being used as a companion.

"Prudence is fitting in nicely," Aunt Catherine informed Fitzwilliam, unconcerned that her words could be heard. "We hardly notice Mrs. Jenkinson's absence at all."

Fitzwilliam rolled his eyes at the crass comment but used the opportunity to bring his cousin into the conversation. "Do you live in Manchester, Cousin?"

"No. Just on the outskirts. A little place called Stretford," she said. "Although the city seems to grow daily, so I'm sure that soon our house will be absorbed into the spread."

"Her father contacted me a few years ago to say that he thought she should spend some time with her mother's family," Lady Catherine informed Fitzwilliam.

"How many years ago?" Fitzwilliam asked incredulously. His aunt couldn't hold her tongue about anything, except when it came to poorer relations, it seemed.

"Oh, about ten. Soon after her mother died," Lady Catherine shrugged.

"I'm sorry we did not know about you then," Fitzwilliam apologised to Prudence. "I know Darcy and myself would have liked to be acquainted with you."

"He had Georgiana to bring up, and now he has his hands full with that family he insisted on connecting himself to."

"The Bennet family are a delight to be around. Most of them," Fitzwilliam said with grin. "Every family has the sort of relations who one would wish to hide from society."

"I am to be yours, Cousin," Prudence said, but her twinkling eyes laughed their understanding of his comment. "My Papa had ideas that I would want to be a genteel lady and be brought out in society. I have never aspired to that lifestyle. I'm happy with my upbringing, although it is nice to meet some of my mother's family. The older I get, the more curious I am, especially as father always said I resembled that side of the family more than his."

"It was impossible for me to sponsor you for a season with Anne being so ill," Lady Catherine defended her actions. "And how could I introduce the daughter of a cotton-spinner into the finest society?"

"Aunt!" Fitzwilliam hissed, mortified that she could be so rude

"Don't trouble yourself on my account," Prudence said to Fitzwilliam. "When you have spent as much time around a cotton mill as I have, you would realise I've heard far worse insults."

"Have you really?" Anne was stirred into asking.

Turning to her cousin, Prudence smiled. "Oh yes. Mill girls work from ten years old. They're as tough as the clogs they wear on their feet, and if they have an opinion, they say it. Mind you, if you are in a spot of bother, they will be the first to offer help. They're the kind of people you want on your side in any situation."

"It sounds an utterly barbaric place," Lady Catherine shuddered. "How your mother could sink to such depths, I will never understand."

Fitzwilliam noticed the darkening of Prudence's expression, even if his aunt did not, but it passed quickly enough, to be replaced by a bland gaze. He suspected his cousin was restraining herself in their aunt's presence — something he could empathise with completely.

"My mother, because of love, willingly joined a community that welcomed her wholeheartedly. She was more than happy, working by my father's side until the day she died," Prudence said firmly, unable to let her aunt's comment go completely unchallenged.

"We should all be allowed to marry for love," Fitzwilliam interjected.

"Are you a romantic, Cousin?" Prudence asked. Her laughing look returned as quickly as it had disappeared.

"I'm too poor to be so," Fitzwilliam shrugged. "A second son needs to find a rich wife or a career."

Raising an eyebrow, Prudence assessed him. "And which are you choosing?"

"I've picked a career that doesn't pay as much as my tastes would wish."

"Where I come from, we cut our cloth accordingly. People live within their means," Prudence said.

"We have a duty to keep tradesmen in work," Lady Catherine interpolated. "What would happen if everyone were frugal? I could employ half the servants I do, and many families in the village would suffer as a result. Is that what you would want?"

"Not at all. It's to your credit to be so generous in employing the numbers you do," Prudence said quickly. "My objection is spending when the bills can't be paid. That can result in real hardship for families while they wait to see if the gentry pay their debts. I would suggest that the tradespeople are in a far more precarious situation than those creating the debt."

Fitzwilliam stepped in quickly. He could see the thunderous expression on his aunt's face and knew without doubt, if the argument continued, it would not end well for Prudence. That his aunt didn't like to be disagreed with was obvious to anyone who came in contact with her. She would have no compunction in sending his cousin away, returning her to the wilds of Manchester, which was a characteristic of Lady Catherine that Prudence clearly hadn't quite realised yet.

"Have you seen much of the Collinses since you arrived?" he asked quickly.

"Yes. Aunt Catherine has kindly invited them a few times," Prudence said with a knowing look at Fitzwilliam's tactic. "Mrs. Collins is a very pleasant lady."

"Yes. She's Mrs. Darcy's best friend," Fitzwilliam said. "I will walk over to the parsonage tomorrow. Would you like to join me, Cousin?"

"I like to spend time with Anne in the mornings," Prudence said. "But if you intend setting out after that, I will gladly accompany you."

"I've told her to get as much fresh air as she can while she is down here. Best to get some clean air to chase away the muck of the city," Lady Catherine said.

Fitzwilliam decided it was going to be a long visit.

Chapter 2

Fitzwilliam was happy to wait until Prudence and Anne returned from their carriage ride. He had spent the evening at his aunt's side, and only after she retired, was he able to indulge in enough brandy to deaden the headache caused by her close proximity. How he had missed Darcy!

Coming downstairs with a slightly fuddled head, he smiled at the two young women entering the front hallway. Anne was walking better, more upright, and she was smiling again, something that hadn't happened much once her mother had appeared the day before.

Bowing to them both, he smiled. "Would you both like to accompany me to Hunsford parsonage? I am happy to have each of my arms escort a pretty lady."

Prudence looked at Anne and shook her head in despair. "Is he always so full of flummery?"

Anne looked at Fitzwilliam with a little trepidation, but smiled at Prudence. "Sometimes. Yes. Mostly."

Fitzwilliam let out a crack of laughter. "I like this new Anne," he said with a smile.

Blushing, Anne smiled at the compliment. "So do I. But please forgive me. I don't think a walk would do me good. I still get quite tired. I am happy to sit in the library until Mother comes downstairs. Prudence has given me some novels, and I am enjoying them."

"Oh, really? Another secret from Lady Catherine?"

"No. We just haven't mentioned the fact. The books are quite visible," Prudence pointed out.

"My aunt never enters the library," Fitzwilliam said with a smile.

"But she could," Prudence countered.

"About as likely as me making general."

"How disappointing. I thought my new family were all destined for great things," Prudence said.

"Unfortunately, most second sons hang on to the tailcoats of the other members of the family." Fitzwilliam shrugged. "Enjoy your books, Anne. We shall seek you out when we return."

"Have a lovely time," Anne said with a wave and walked towards the library.

Fitzwilliam offered his arm to Prudence, and she laid her hand on it before they exited the house. Turning towards the path that cut through the grounds, giving the neighbours a useful shortcut to the parsonage, he strolled at an easy pace.

"You've done wonders for Anne," he stated as soon as they were out of earshot of the house.

"She was not hard to persuade into more activity," Prudence said. "I felt so sorry for her when I first arrived."

"Yes. To be sickly with an overbearing mother cannot have been easy. The whole family has sympathised with her situation, but spending two weeks with our aunt will have shown you how dashed awkward it is trying to interfere on Anne's behalf," he admitted.

"I think she isn't as ill as everyone else thinks," Prudence said thoughtfully. "She has been taught to believe that she's unwell, which has influenced her and everyone around her in the way they treat her and how she behaves."

"I'm glad she is responding to you."

"We are of a similar age. She is only a few years older than I."

"I still think of her as being very young," Fitzwilliam admitted.

"Papa still considers me a bantling," Prudence smiled.

"Do you see much of each other? I'm led to believe that the hours are long, and the work is hard."

"Are we allowed to talk of such crude subjects?" Prudence teased. "I've been told expressly by our aunt that to talk of being in trade is not de rigueur."

"Oh dear. She does have a way with words." Fitzwilliam grimaced. "It isn't quite the thing to talk about when one is in society. Aunt Catherine is right in that regard. In recent years I have fought with men from all backgrounds, and I am not so high in the instep as to lord it over anyone. Plus, I'm genuinely interested."

Prudence smiled. "In that case, yes, the hours are long. Papa works extremely hard, but he has always been committed to our family and the area in which we live. Very often people seek his advice on any number of issues, and he always welcomes them. He's very personable. I think that is what attracted my mother to him."

"How did they meet?"

"Papa was on a trip to Derbyshire when mother was visiting her sister, Mrs. Darcy. They came across each other in the village of Lambton."

"Ah, I see. That makes sense. I wondered how the connection had been made. We are not the largest of families, so apart from visiting London, we do not travel around as much as other, larger families who seem to spread across the country. And with so few relatives, it is a real pity we didn't know about you sooner. I wish Aunt

24

Catherine had told us about you when your father first wrote to her."

"I disagree."

"Really? Why?" Fitzwilliam asked in surprise.

"I would have been ten years younger and far more easily intimidated," Prudence admitted. "Now I can enjoy my time with Aunt Catherine. I doubt I would have done when I was fifteen."

"I suppose so. Although I am not sure when she will stop intimidating me. I usually hide behind my cousin, Darcy, when we visit. I'm deeply disappointed that he chose to remain with Elizabeth, even though the baby is due within the next three months or so."

"How selfish they are, leaving you to stand alone. Never mind. You can hide behind me," Prudence offered. "I'll protect you."

"Thank you. I no longer have anything to fear," Fitzwilliam said with a smile. "I hope you will also protect me against Mr. Collins."

"Oh no," Prudence said quickly. "You are on your own where he's concerned!"

*

Mr. Collins was everything Fitzwilliam disliked in a person: pompous, silly, and conceited. On the visit, which was occurring after a long absence by Fitzwilliam, he was able to add narrow-minded to his list of the man's faults.

He was within the parsonage walls for only ten minutes before he wanted to punch the clergyman.

"Lady Catherine has been so magnanimous in welcoming Miss Bamber into the fold," Mr. Collins stated as soon as his wife, Charlotte, had taken Prudence to show her a quilt she'd completed. Mr. Collins had waited long enough for the ladies to be out of earshot before he turned the subject to Prudence.

"Let's not forget she needed a companion for my cousin, Anne. I do not think her actions were completely selfless," Fitzwilliam pointed out, his tone brusque, which Mr. Collins failed to notice.

"And what an honour it is to be chosen as companion for Miss De Bourgh. It can only be of benefit to Miss Bamber, extending her experience in such a way. Why, she is sure to secure a fine position after carrying out her duties for Lady Catherine. Is there any higher recommendation than that of Lady Catherine De Bourgh? I think you would struggle to find one," Mr. Collins said.

His words annoyed Fitzwilliam unaccountably. "Has she expressed any desire to be a governess or companion after her visit to Rosings has ended?"

"Well, no. I don't think so. But Lady Catherine has said that she will offer to find Miss Bamber a suitable position somewhere nearby, so Lady Catherine can keep a weather eye on her. Which after the history and the beginning Miss Bamber has had to endure can only be of benefit. I am truly in awe of Lady Catherine's condescension and welcome after a breach in familial relations. It shows just how great a lady she is."

"Until she tires of my cousin and sends her back to Manchester," Fitzwilliam muttered darkly, knowing how his aunt's favour could soon change.

"Not at all. I think she will be content, knowing that she has done her sister a great service in setting up her daughter for her future life." Mr. Collins defended his patroness. "It is a real effort in bringing her back into civilised society."

"By setting me up to work in another household?" Prudence asked as she walked into the drawing room. Charlotte's flushed cheeks showed they had heard enough of the conversation for her to be wishing they'd spent longer out of the room.

"It will be a respectable household, of that you can be assured, Miss Bamber." Mr. Collins smiled.

"I would expect nothing else *if* I were to seek such a position. A pity I won't be taking up my aunt's ever-so-kind offer," Prudence responded, steel in her now stormy grey eyes.

"But my dear Miss Bamber, what could be better than leaving the grime of Manchester behind? I have heard reports it's quite an unhealthy place to live," Mr. Collins said.

"Don't believe everything you hear," Prudence responded.

Fitzwilliam stood, bowing to Charlotte. "Mrs. Collins, let us leave you in peace. I am sure our aunt is expecting our return by now."

Nodding in understanding, Charlotte said her goodbyes and squeezed Prudence's hand in apology.

When the door of the parsonage was closed behind them, Fitzwilliam had to hurry to catch-up with Prudence. He didn't say anything until they were in the confines of the Rosings parkland, and then he reached out with his hand and stayed Prudence's progress.

"Whoa there!" He smiled. "Let's slow down a little. There is no need for us to march back."

Prudence turned to face him, her eyes blazing. "Who would do that?"

"Do what?"

"Decide on a person's future and then tell it to other people as if it's an agreed prospect?" Prudence asked.

"Ah. Aunt Catherine. I was not sure there if your anger was aimed at Mr. Collins or our aunt."

"Mr. Collins is just repeating what he has heard. He hasn't the intelligence to form his own opinions." Prudence dismissed the clergyman in two short sentences. "He is so in awe of Aunt Catherine that he'll agree with anything and everything she says."

"He does, and he will."

"Exactly. But she, she has no right deciding on my future! As if I would give her permission to help me," Prudence said forcefully.

"In her way, she is trying to help," Fitzwilliam said gently.

"I do not need her help, or anyone else's, and the quicker you lot understand that, the better for us all."

"You lot?" Fitzwilliam asked with a raised eyebrow.

Prudence clenched her fists. "You know who I mean. The type of person who thinks they are doing the best for the little people in the world by deciding what's best for them. Do you realise how arrogant and patronising that is?"

"Every landowner has a responsibility to his or her tenants," Fitzwilliam said.

"I am not one of those. I have never asked Aunt Catherine's opinion on anything to do with my life or my future. Nor would I. Ever."

"I'm gathering that. Take heart. She tried to interfere with Darcy's marriage, and he is the owner of one of the largest estates in Derbyshire, so you are in good company."

Prudence narrowed her eyes at him. "Yet I am the poor relation, so I should be grateful of her condescension?"

Holding up his hands, Fitzwilliam stepped away slightly. "I never suggested that, nor thought it."

"Is that because you are a decent sort, or just too lazy as a second son?" Prudence asked, her anger replaced with a twinkle of amusement.

"Definitely the latter," Fitzwilliam answered.

"I thought that might be the case. Does nothing ruffle you deeply? Are you never thrown into a passion?"

"It would seem you do enough of that for the both of us," Fitzwilliam responded.

"Nodcock." Prudence insulted him good-naturedly. "I can see now why you're unmarried. You will not stir yourself enough to entice the women you come into contact with."

"True. Although in my defence, I have little to recommend me to young women who have independent fortunes, other than my charm, wit, and personality, of course. These features leave a lot to be desired," Fitzwilliam said, exaggeratedly pointing at his face, which was being pulled into a ludicrous expression.

Prudence laughed. "You are ungentlemanly, sir! You should have let me wallow in my anger rather than diverting me."

"Then my ears would have been hurting from your rantings. As they are still stinging from Aunt Catherine's monologues of last night, I beseech you to have pity. I rely on you providing an escape, not taking over where our aunt left off!"

"You brute," Prudence smiled. "In my defence I have obviously inherited my temper from my mother's side of the family."

"The female side of your mother's side," Fitzwilliam reasoned.

Chapter 3

The following morning, Fitzwilliam rode out with the ladies, he on horseback while they were in a gig. He was surprised when Anne took the reins.

"Are you a proficient horsewoman now, Anne? Is this yet another hidden talent you have kept from us?"

"No," Anne flushed. "But father did give me some lessons before he died. It was so long ago I never thought I'd remember, but Prudence spent time refreshing my knowledge."

"I am pleased to hear it," Fitzwilliam admitted. It was as if he were seeing Anne for the first time. "And who taught you, Cousin?" he asked of Prudence.

"We might live in an industrial city, but we aren't savages, you know," Prudence responded.

"That's a disappointment, indeed," Fitzwilliam replied.

Prudence shook her head. "You have a fine horse there, Cousin. I now understand a little of why you are in need of further funds."

"So, you know good horseflesh, do you?"

"My father is a believer that, whether you are a girl or boy, you should know your way around things to reduce the chance of being swindled. He is fond of saying that it's stood him in good stead. I think the reality is, he's treated me more like a boy than a girl because he was disappointed when I was born," Prudence said with a smile.

"I think father was dismayed to have a girl in my case, too," Anne admitted shyly.

"Well, I for one am glad you are not, or I'd be surrounded by blockheaded men, if our Cousin Fitzwilliam is anything to go by," Prudence said quickly.

"I would love to be there when you finally get to meet Darcy," Fitzwilliam said with a grin. "I can't wait to see the sparks fly."

"Will he put me in my place as Aunt Catherine tries?"

"Oh, no," Anne said quickly. "Darcy is not like mother, but he can be a little terrifying sometimes. Not so much now I'm not in fear of having to marry him."

"Is he a gargoyle to look at? Would he have frightened you to gaze at him every day?" Prudence smiled.

"No. He is certainly handsome," Anne admitted. "Just a little awe-inspiring."

"I am even more curious to meet my cousin. He sounds intriguing."

"I'm sure you will meet him one day, but he is not at his best when visiting Rosings," Fitzwilliam admitted. "He also suffered from Aunt Catherine's insistence that you two were to marry," he said, looking at Anne.

"She was very determined," Anne admitted with a shudder.

"And Darcy was equally as fixed on not being persuaded," Fitzwilliam smiled at his cousin. "You had no real need to fear."

"Mother does get her way so often, though. I was very relieved to hear he was betrothed to Elizabeth."

"Yes. It is a good match in every regard."

"Families are very interesting," Prudence smiled.

"Aren't they just! What other adventures can we have while you're with us?" Fitzwilliam asked of Prudence.

"Are there any dances to attend? I do love dancing," she admitted wistfully.

"Westerham is only five miles away, and they have a monthly assembly," Anne said.

"We should go!" Prudence said.

"Mother would never agree to it. I might catch cold if I were out so late," Anne responded.

"Do you go to assemblies only in the summer?" Prudence asked.

"I don't go at all," Anne admitted.

Prudence exchanged a look with Fitzwilliam but said nothing.

On their return journey, they received a wave from a member of staff who was walking along the lane and who had stopped at the sound of a vehicle approaching. Anne slowed the horses at his greeting.

"Good morning, Mr. Huxley. This is my cousin, Miss Bamber," Anne said, a blush tinging her cheeks. "This is my mother's steward," she said to Prudence.

"Good morning, Miss Anne. It is good to see you outside," Mr. Huxley said. "I'm just making my way to the house to see Lady Catherine now."

"Oh, you won't tell her you have seen me, will you?" Anne panicked.

"Not at all, Miss Anne. No reason to trouble Lady Catherine with such a trifling matter."

"Thank you. That is very kind of you," Anne blushed.

"Mr. Huxley, why don't you take my place?" Prudence said, reaching over and pulling on the reins to make the equipage come to a full stop. "I'm not ready to return to the house quite yet, so I will walk back, and you can ride there." Anne stiffened, but patting her cousin's arm and giving her a reassuring smile, Prudence jumped nimbly onto the ground.

Mr. Huxley immediately came around to the side of the carriage and bowed his head at Prudence. "Thank you, Miss Bamber. I shall enjoy the journey."

"I thought you might," Prudence smiled before she set-off purposely away from the vehicle. Hearing Fitzwilliam speak to Anne, she smiled up at him as he came alongside her still on his mount. "Not playing chaperone?"

Pausing, whilst he dismounted, Fitzwilliam grinned at Prudence. "What mischief are you up to?"

With a feigned innocent look, Prudence batted her eyes. "I have no idea what you mean."

"Come now. You're playing it too brown."

"Oh, all right. Anne might have mentioned that she thinks Mr. Huxley is handsome." Prudence shrugged. "And he seemed very keen to take up my offer, so I think there might be a mutual attraction there."

Fitzwilliam laughed. "If you think Aunt Catherine would consider for a moment a romance between those two, you have learned nothing since your arrival in Kent."

"If they were to fall in love with each other, why not?" Prudence shrugged.

"The heiress of Rosings, married to the steward? Now, that would cause gossip," Fitzwilliam smiled. "Aunt Catherine would have apoplexy."

"People should be allowed to marry whomever they wish, especially when there are no constraints such as money. Anne will have enough funds to keep them, and Mr. Huxley obviously works hard for the benefit of Rosings. It's a perfect match in my view."

"Seriously, Cousin. Even if Anne wished it to happen, she'd never have the courage to stand up to her mother to achieve what she wished. An encouragement of the scheme by any of us would only end with Anne suffering," Fitzwilliam cautioned.

"Then the poor girl is doomed to end her days lonely and unloved, for I cannot imagine Anne wishing to marry someone who is of a similar personality to Darcy. He might not be as bad as Anne makes out, but to her, he is terrifying. Not a good prospect in a marriage."

"I am sure Aunt Catherine will have started to think of a different husband for Anne, now that she has had to accept that Darcy will not be marrying her."

"How cold for all the parties involved."

"It is how things are sometimes. A business transaction to join lands or secure wealth or heritage. Love matches happen but aren't the case in every marriage."

"You have said that you are one of those who cannot marry as you wish?"

"Not if I want a good lifestyle," Fitzwilliam admitted, but for the first time the thought of seeking out an heiress and marrying her for her money didn't sound as appealing as it had.

"I hope to marry for love, which is why, at five and twenty, I am single," Prudence smiled.

"Does your father wish you to marry? Most girls have married by the time they're one and twenty at the latest. Many marry straight out of the schoolroom. Any older and they're in danger of being on the shelf."

"Goodness me! What sort of a society do you belong to?" Prudence exclaimed. "I admit many women do tend to marry by the ages you mentioned, but I am not the only one of my peer group who is unwed. I don't feel we are cast off as unmarriageable quite so quickly as you seem to make out those in your circles are."

"Has your father not encouraged you to find a husband?"

"He wants me to marry one day, but I'm under no pressure from him to do so," Prudence admitted. "It seems his ideas of my securing at least a viscount will come to naught though." She laughed. "I did not realise I was an old maid. I thought I had years yet before that label was attached to me."

"Your father wanted you to come to Rosings in order to secure a title?" Fitzwilliam asked in disbelief.

"Oh, take that expression off your face!" Prudence laughed. "I'm not a deluded fool and neither is Papa. We were funning with each other when he mentioned it. He had his reasons for contacting Aunt Catherine all those years ago, and I have my own reasons for visiting since our aunt issued her invitation. Neither involve securing a viscount, or any other title, for that matter."

"I see," Fitzwilliam said. He couldn't understand the feeling of relief that swept through him, but knew he was unaccountably happy at her words. It must be to do with her not being disappointed. That was it. His concern was for his cousin, wasn't it?

Prudence accompanied Fitzwilliam to the stables, chatting as he tended his horse, and they entered the house laughing at something or other. Lady Catherine was leaving the study with Mr. Huxley in her wake.

"Good afternoon, Aunt," Fitzwilliam said amiably. "And how are you this fine day?"

Lady Catherine responded with a harrumph before leaving her member of staff and leading the way into the morning room, indicating to the pair that they should follow.

Both would have liked to change their outerwear, but followed meekly, Prudence gathering the skirts of her riding habit over her arm.

When the threesome entered the room, they saw that Anne was seated on one of the chairs near the fire, rubbing her hands in front of the flames.

"Do you ail, Anne?" Lady Catherine asked.

"No. Not at all. I'm just warming my hands," she said with a reassuring smile, but there was a wariness in her expression.

"I expect you to ensure Anne has everything she needs to prevent her coming down with a cold," Lady Catherine said to Prudence.

"I would not insult Anne's intelligence by trying to tell her what to do and what not to do. There is very little difference in our ages. She would likely box my ears if I tried," Prudence responded lightly, taking a seat closer to the window to try to avoid the oppressive heat of the room.

Lady Catherine glared at her niece, but before she had a chance to respond to Prudence's comment, Fitzwilliam intervened. "Aunt, I'd love the opportunity to show off you and my two lovely cousins at the next assembly in Westerham. When is it to take place?"

"It would not be appropriate to take Anne. She would be fatigued because of the excursion."

"I would not, Mother, and it would be nice to go," Anne said quickly, looking daunted at disagreeing with her mother but gaining encouragement by the reassuring look Prudence sent in her direction at the words.

"Have you put these foolish ideas into Anne's head?" Lady Catherine snapped at Prudence.

"Possibly," Prudence admitted. "I asked if there was any opportunity for dancing in the area. Although I wouldn't want Anne's health to suffer as a result of my urge to dance."

"Perhaps I could escort you, Cousin?" Fitzwilliam asked of Prudence, his eyes laughing with mischief. "That way, Aunt Catherine and Anne could remain at Rosings, and we could tell them of who was in attendance and who danced with whom."

There was a slight pause while Lady Catherine looked with narrowed eyes at Fitzwilliam, as if assessing the seriousness of his words. She had seated herself in the largest chair in the room, her usual position, and she fiddled with the folds of her gown.

"We shall attend the next assembly," she said finally.

The three occupants in the room breathed a sigh of relief.

"But I don't expect you to dance, Anne," came the warning.

"Of course not, Mother," Anne replied obediently, but her eyes reflected the excitement she felt in attending an evening's entertainment.

"If I could secure the first two dances with you, Cousin?" Fitzwilliam asked Prudence.

"That would be delightful."

*

Anne was sitting on the chaise longue in Prudence's bedchamber. Lady Catherine had put Prudence in Mrs. Jenkinson's room, the latter's possessions being banished to the attic until her return. The room was positioned at the rear of the house, overlooking the kitchen gardens. It was the smallest chamber on the floor, but was a floor below the servants' rooms, acknowledging the elevated status of a companion. Anne could often be found in the chamber since her cousin's arrival, enjoying the cosy room and warm fire.

Prudence had been teaching Anne a few dance steps, in the hope that her cousin would be able to dance at least one dance.

"It is very tiring," Anne admitted, having needed to sit down to catch her breath.

"You aren't used to a great deal of exercise, so it will be hard at the beginning. What you need is someone as understanding as Mr. Huxley to stand up with. And then if you should tire, he could take you out of the dance without a fuss being made," Prudence coaxed.

"Mother would never agree to my dancing, but especially not with Mr. Huxley," Anne said, aghast at the thought.

"That's a shame. You should be able to dance with whomever you wish."

"I envy you. You seem to do whatever you want," Anne said.

"Not at all. I have constraints just as everyone else does. It is just that I've been brought up to think most things are achievable, and I haven't got a mother with such steadfast opinions. I have run wild since my own mother died," Prudence admitted.

"You managed to persuade Mother to take us to an assembly. That is an achievement indeed."

"I think that had to do more with our cousin's words than mine," Prudence acknowledged.

"He's very good."

"Yes, he is a good sort," Prudence said. The new cousin was becoming far more important to her than she could have supposed at the start of her introduction into her mother's family.

"And single," Anne said with a sly look.

"Just you watch what you are suggesting, Miss De Bourgh," Prudence said primly. "Our cousin is as likely to fix his interest on me as you are to stand up with Mr. Huxley."

"Maybe a dance with Mr. Huxley is not so unachievable after all," Anne said with a smile.

"Pfft. You have claws, Cousin, and are a minx to boot. This meek and mild exterior is just to fool us all."

"I have no idea what you mean," Anne replied.

Chapter 4

Walking downstairs, Fitzwilliam noticed the door to the study was ajar, and catching a glimpse of a muslin skirt, he changed direction and entered the room.

Prudence was standing, looking at the portrait hanging over the fireplace. She had a wistful air about her but smiled in welcome at Fitzwilliam.

"Ah, you are looking at the three sisters," Fitzwilliam said. The portrait was done when the sisters were all under twenty years of age. They were gathered together, the painting just showing their shoulders and heads, and although they were not smiling, there was a twinkle in one of the sister's eyes.

"Did you know that my mother was in this portrait when it was first painted?" Prudence asked.

"Really? No. I have never heard that before," Fitzwilliam admitted.

"Anne said Aunt Catherine admitted to the fact when Anne asked if there were any portraits of my mother. Our grandfather had this painting altered after Mama married Papa and destroyed any paintings of just Mama."

"I realise you must remember your mother clearly," Fitzwilliam said. "Have you any likenesses of her?"

"Oh, yes. Father was besotted with her, and Mama's picture is in all forms at home. There are a few of us together, which I now treasure even more."

Fitzwilliam frowned as he considered the painting. Portraits cost money. Lots of it, depending on the painter. He was surprised a cotton worker could afford more than one portrait. It niggled at him, along with other inconsistencies about Prudence. He was distracted from his ponderings by a sigh from her.

"What is it?" he asked gently.

"I would have liked to have seen them together," Prudence admitted. "I do not resemble Mama — or Papa for that matter. I have always wondered where I fitted in, if that makes sense? I obviously know where I belong, and I am happy with my life. Don't misunderstand me. But there was always a part missing. A part I was curious about."

"I suppose there would be. Your father clearly understood, hence his wishing for you to get to know us."

"Yes. He is an astute man and a considerate one. I would have understood if he'd never wished me to be in contact with mother's family, but he was always aware that there were questions bubbling inside me."

"You are very like Darcy's mother," Fitzwilliam said. "I actually thought that from the moment I saw you."

It was Prudence's turn to frown at the painting. "Do you think so? To me, she is the prettiest of the sisters, which is utterly appalling of me to say as one of those is your own mother!"

Laughing, Fitzwilliam folded his arms in mock anger. "I am disgusted at your insult. Be gone! Back to the north, wench!"

"Buffoon!"

"My mother would love to have met you before now," Fitzwilliam said. "I think our grandfather was of similar characteristics as Aunt Catherine. What he said was never challenged by his daughters. I wish she were close by so I could ask — so you could ask — all the questions Aunt Catherine would never answer. One day I am sure you will meet."

"Yes. I foolishly tried to ask question after question when I first arrived, expecting that Aunt Catherine would fill all the gaps for me. Unfortunately, whenever I brought up the subject of my mother, all I received was either a scolding or a lecture about my mother's actions in eloping." Prudence grimaced. "It is a shame that she is only remembered for one tiny moment in her life."

"That happens very often, I think. Particularly where characters like Aunt Catherine are concerned. Cousin Elizabeth will always be too lowly birthed for Darcy, no matter how well she is at being mistress of Pemberley, which is larger than Rosings. Anne will always be a fragile little thing because she was sickly as a child. Aunt Catherine seizes on the thing that she can repine over again and again and use to her advantage. It isn't a becoming trait," Fitzwilliam said.

"No."

"But you are like Darcy's mother. And yes, that means I consider you very pretty."

Prudence flushed a little, but laughed it off. "As I have said before, I know exactly where I stand with regard to looks. I am all angles and sharpness."

Fitzwilliam swung around and caught hold of Prudence's hands. When she was facing him, warily regarding him, he released her. Using his fingertips, he traced the contours of her face. "You have laughing eyes that sparkle beautifully. Your cheekbones are high and accentuate your slim features. Your lips are always ready to smile; their curve upwards is testament to that. Yes, you are very pretty."

Having stilled at the most intimate exploration of her face, Prudence's eyes had widened as she watched Fitzwilliam's serious expression as he described her. Swallowing at their closeness and the feelings the experience caused, she tried to think of a retort that would turn the situation into a funny one. Unfortunately, her brain stopped working, and she was finding it difficult to speak.

Fitzwilliam seemed to gather himself when his fingers reached the curve of her chin. Tenderly smiling at her, he reached over and kissed her nose. "You are beautiful. Never forget that."

Turning, he walked out of the room, silently cursing the fact that he had not grabbed her and kissed her fully and wondering how the devil he was going to figure out a way to avoid contact with her. He was being affected like he had never been affected by anyone before. It was extremely worrying and irresistible at the same time.

*

The following morning Prudence settled into the wing-backed chair, a cushion tucked under her arm, propping up the book she was reading. Her feet were curled underneath her, her satin slippers on the carpet.

She looked up quickly as the door opened, ready to alter her stance if needed, but relaxed when she saw Fitzwilliam enter the room.

"Am I disturbing you?" Fitzwilliam asked as he closed the door behind him.

"Not at all. I should say I am reading something educational, but I am not. Anne told me that I must read this novel. Miss Goode recommended it to her, and she contrived to have it delivered to the house without Aunt Catherine finding out," she explained.

Fitzwilliam laughed. "I'm still surprised that I am seeing a whole other side to Anne than what I have been used to. She is becoming quite rebellious."

"In her own quiet way. I think it's since she no longer has the threat of marrying Cousin Darcy."

"I think it is more to do with a certain rebel from Manchester." Fitzwilliam flicked out the tails of his frock coat and sat on the chair opposite Prudence.

"I'm not in the slightest bit rebellious," Prudence laughed.

"I'm afraid I cannot believe such an outrageous lie."

"You do me a great disservice," Prudence scolded. "I shall have you know that I was brought up every bit the polite miss."

"Of course you were. A pity your teacher did not realise there was a streak of mischief underneath that polite façade."

"Yes. Papa always hoped it would be something my governess could overcome, but I was a lost cause."

Fitzwilliam frowned slightly. She'd had a governess. That was something he hadn't expected to hear, and he wished to question her further. Only his reluctance to begin to sound like his aunt prevented him from asking other questions.

He saw Prudence watching him and suspected she was aware of his inner thoughts. He flushed a little but smiled at her. "I'm interested to hear about Manchester and where you live."

"I would imagine Manchester is like no place you have visited."

"I spend the season in London, which is a larger city," Fitzwilliam pointed out.

"But do you spend your time in the gardens and refined houses, or do you explore the areas where the business is carried out? Where the real work takes place?" The questions were asked with a laugh, for she was fully aware of what his answer would be.

"I have not had a completely privileged lifestyle," Fitzwilliam answered. His tone was defensive.

"I know," Prudence said, immediately contrite. "We had some soldiers returning to our area. Their injuries are terrible, and some are reduced to begging because they cannot work. It is pitiful to see."

"They should be helped. They gave up their livelihoods to protect this country, and we repay them by forcing them to beg and be out of work? It's a disgrace!" Fitzwilliam looked angry, standing and walking to the decanter. His shoulders stiff, he poured himself a large brandy and took a swig. "No one who willingly went onto those battlefields should have to work another day, let alone beg for their existence. No one in these fine houses understands what it was like. What it was really like."

He had not turned back to Prudence, but she moved over to him, placing her arm gently on his. He tensed under her touch but didn't pull away.

"I agree completely. We have organisations that try to help. I'm involved with some of them. We do what we can, but I know it is not enough."

"You are very good to give up your time."

"It is the least I can do. I'm sorry to have upset you. I go blundering in without thinking. Now you can see why I am such a lost cause in my father's eyes," Prudence said with a slight smile, but she rubbed her hand gently along his arm.

Fitzwilliam looked down at her. She was smaller than he, but only just. She had struck him from the first moment he had met her as a capable woman. To see compassion and understanding in her eyes was even more compelling. He rarely spoke to anyone about his experiences.

"I sent so many to their deaths," he said quietly.

"No. Napoleon did that. You sent men to defend our country, and the other countries of Europe, from a tyrant."

"It didn't feel like that then, or now. I know the names of every single man who was injured in my regiment or who didn't come back."

Prudence rested her head on Fitzwilliam's shoulder in an act of empathy. "It is to your credit that you do so," she said.

"I sometimes feel guilty that I survived. I mean who would miss me if I had not returned? A handful of people perhaps, but there were men with children and wives who were lost on the battlefield. That does not seem fair."

Feeling a chill at his words, Prudence kept her voice calm. "Everyone is important. It is wrong to put one person above another."

"Perhaps. It is just that when I look back — oh you've caught me in a maudlin mood!" Fitzwilliam laughed. He bent down slightly and kissed the top of Prudence's head affectionately before moving away from her.

Prudence moved back to her seat, accepting his change of tone, not interpreting the kiss as anything other than a show of part affection, part apology for his more serious mood. She felt sorry that he was the one always seen as the jovial one when it was clear to her that he suffered, and his words had confirmed that.

"Were you looking to read? Or were you just seeking an escape?" Prudence asked, changing the subject.

Fitzwilliam grinned. "An escape. Could you not see the hunted expression I wore when I entered?"

"Aunt Catherine could have followed you in here, and we both would have been caught."

"Better to have a partner in crime than to face her wrath alone."

"Coward."

"Completely, when my aunt is involved. Shall we take a turn around the gardens?"

"We risk being caught if we enter the hallway," Prudence pointed out.

"But not if we escape through the window," Fitzwilliam said, moving over to one of the three full-length windows in the library. Unhooking the catch, he swung the door open. "Ready for a real escape, Cousin?"

"You are incorrigible," Prudence said, but the book was forgotten as she walked towards Fitzwilliam.

Offering his hand, he held tight until she'd stepped into the open. "Are you warm enough?" he asked. "I should have contrived a way of obtaining at least a shawl for you."

Prudence shook her head in the negative. "No. You forget I live in the north. It is positively balmy here."

"I think you fun with us much of the time," Fitzwilliam said. "I hardly know when to take you seriously about your life back home. My instinct is to think most of the time you are bamboozling us."

"I do not! I have every respect for all my new relations and would not tease you so." Prudence defended herself, but her smile was mischievous.

"And that comment is a prime example of what I mean! You are a minx, but beware! For I am on to you."

Prudence laughed. "You, sir, are a rogue."

"And you, dear Cousin, are quite possibly the most intriguing woman I have ever met."

Fitzwilliam's words increased Prudence's guilt, but she tried to push it aside. She would tell him of her situation soon. She wanted to be honest with him more than anything, but she was becoming more worried about the reaction her words would cause. There should have been truthfulness from the start. He was suspicious of her. She could see that, and needing to be frank with him was becoming more and more important to her.

They strolled about the gardens, thoroughly enjoying each other's company, until Fitzwilliam caught Prudence shivering.

"Oh, blast it! You are cold! Why didn't you say?" he asked in some consternation, immediately shrugging himself out of his frock coat.

"Do not concern yourself. It is only now that I've started to feel a chill. I have been enjoying myself too much to return to the house before."

Fitzwilliam wrapped his frock coat around Prudence's shoulders. "Here. Take this. I too have been enjoying myself, but I insist we return. I'd be mortified if you caught a chill."

Prudence relished the feel of the still warm coat. It felt delightful to be encompassed within the fine material. She wondered if it was the quality of the coat or the fact that it was his that made her feel quite heated as they returned to the house.

Entering the hallway, both let out a silent groan when they were faced with Lady Catherine, coming down the stairs.

Their aunt paused mid-step. "What is this?" she demanded staring at Prudence wrapped in Fitzwilliam's clothing.

"We have been for a walk and realised belatedly it was becoming cold," Fitzwilliam explained, accepting his frock coat from Prudence, who had immediately relinquished it on seeing Lady Catherine.

"You have been outside without bonnet, gloves, or spencer?" Lady Catherine asked Prudence.

"It was a spur of the moment decision," Prudence admitted.

"It was my fault, Aunt. I persuaded my cousin to leave what she was doing and go into the garden through one of the windows. I did not give her the opportunity to retrieve her outerwear. I should have done so, and I apologise for it," Fitzwilliam said, with a slight bow of his head towards Prudence.

"I enjoyed the excursion," Prudence admitted with a smile.

Lady Catherine narrowed her eyes at her niece. "That is conduct that is not becoming of a relative of mine."

"I am sorry, Aunt," Prudence said demurely.

"It was my doing entirely," Fitzwilliam interjected.

"It is Prudence's responsibility to know what she should and should not do. How can she hope to improve herself if she continues to behave like a hoyden?"

"Aunt! For goodness sake! We went into the garden!" Fitzwilliam snapped, probably for the first time, at his aunt.

"It is easy for you to say that, but she must remember her place. It is far too easy to be condemned for one's actions. My connections to her won't always protect her," Lady Catherine said.

"Oh, dear Lord!" Fitzwilliam said.

"It does not matter, Cousin," Prudence said quietly. "Aunt, please forgive my lapse of judgement. It will not happen again."

"I am glad to hear it. Now I suggest you go into the library and spend a half hour on reading a sermon. I can choose one for you if you like."

"No. Thank you. I can choose a suitable sermon myself," Prudence said quickly. "And remove the evidence of my novel," she whispered to Fitzwilliam as she passed him on the way to the library.

Hearing a choke caused by her words, Prudence tried to suppress the smile on her lips, but by the glare she received from her aunt, she wasn't convinced she'd achieved it.

Chapter 5

The evening of the assembly soon came around, and although Lady Catherine had hinted at cancelling the trip a few times over the passing days, Fitzwilliam had always countered that he would still accompany Prudence, using Mrs. Collins as a chaperone. As Lady Catherine was loath to be excluded from any activity and Fitzwilliam's threat hung over her head, there was never any real danger of the trip not going ahead.

Anne and Prudence entered the drawing room together. Fitzwilliam was standing at the fireplace and turned to greet the ladies. He faltered at the sight of them framed in the doorway.

Dressed in a pale pink satin with organza overlay and decorated with tiny embroidered flowers, Anne looked almost ethereal with her pale complexion and slight frame. Her brown locks had been fixed in a softer style than she normally wore, curls framing her face. Her colour was heightened, and she smiled shyly at her cousin.

"Anne, you look beautiful," Fitzwilliam said, and he meant it. He had never seen her look so well.

"Thank you. Do you think it is too much? It's only a local assembly after all." Anne asked, uncertainty in her voice.

"Not at all!" Fitzwilliam said quickly. "You look perfect, and I only wish I could stand up with you, for I would love to be the one to show you off to the locality."

If Fitzwilliam had been stunned at Anne's appearance, his mouth had gone dry at the sight of Prudence. She wore a rich navy-blue silk dress. It seemed to fall against her tall frame, highlighting her figure to its best effect. Silver lace edged the gown, and a sapphire and silver necklace focused the eyes on the low, but not too revealing, neckline. Her hair was dressed similar to Anne's at the front, but she had left more length at the back, resulting in a cascading tumble of curls. A silver shawl wrapped around her shoulders, and silver gloves contrasted with the dress. She wore no make-up apart from black on her eyelashes and a rich red on her lips. She looked regal and elegant.

"I am to be the envy of every man in the room tonight," he said to Prudence, his voice a little choked.

Prudence smiled, her cheeks colouring slightly but said nothing.

Fitzwilliam wasn't used to being without words, so he was relieved when Lady Catherine followed his cousins into the room. She assessed Anne with approval and then turned her scrutinising gaze onto Prudence.

"That's an expensive dress," she stated.

"Yes. It is," Prudence answered.

"Your father has tried his best to show you in a positive light. It does him credit," Lady Catherine conceded.

"He spoils me."

"The jewels look the real thing. Paste is a wonderful ingredient. Only an expert eye would suspect anything. You will do, and if you continue to please me, I shall allow you to wear some of my own jewels at the next assembly."

Prudence smiled sweetly at her aunt but once more remained silent.

Fitzwilliam wondered at the exchange, always wishing his aunt would be slightly more tactful. He silently commended Prudence's restraint, for he knew she would have made some comment if it had been anyone else uttering the remark.

"Come. We are to collect the Collinses," Lady Catherine said. "I want to hear all about how my instructions on the tenants' homes are being received. I tasked Collins with speaking to them."

"Isn't that a job for your steward?" Fitzwilliam asked.

"Huxley had other jobs to do. He is capable, but I like to keep an eye on what he does."

The three groaned quietly in unison. The journey would be tedious and without the anticipation of an enjoyable evening to look forward to with Mr. Collins and Lady Catherine having a conversation. All of a sudden, five miles in a carriage seemed a very long distance.

*

Entering into the Assembly, Fitzwilliam had an inkling as to the real reason Lady Catherine didn't frequent the assemblies very often. There was a real mixture of people in the room. It was obviously an area without enough families to make the event exclusive to the top of society. There were members from the middle classes, and if his aunt's expression and mutterings were anything to go by, as she surveyed the room, many people of trade.

The arrival of Lady Catherine caused a bit of a stir, and one of the head members of the older families in the area immediately approached the group and bowed deeply over Lady Catherine's hand.

"My lady, it is an honour to see you here. Please, would you join my family? My mother is with us and very much desirous to speak with you."

"Sir James, that would be preferable to joining any other group I can see in this place," Lady Catherine said with a sniff, accepting the proffered arm and being led towards a table at which there was an elderly lady and two younger ones already seated. They were the daughters of Sir James Goode. One was married, but the other was unmarried, pretty, and had the same open character as her father.

The party broke into two natural groups, Lady Catherine, Mr. and Mrs. Collins with Sir James, his elder daughter and her husband, and Sir James's mother. The younger, unmarried members standing to one side. Anne had to concede to her mother's request that she accept a chair, but apart from that, Lady Catherine turned her attention away from the group.

Miss Goode's dance partner collected her in plenty of time for the first dance. When Fitzwilliam offered his hand to Prudence she hesitated.

"We can't leave Anne here alone," she said.

"Oh, yes. Of course, we can't."

"Please do not worry about me. I'm happy to remain here and watch the dancing," Anne said quickly.

"It would be a poor show indeed if we left you without a companion, and I know your mother wouldn't be happy," Prudence said.

"I do not want to join their group, though," Anne said quietly. "I shan't be able to escape for the rest of the evening."

"True," Fitzwilliam mused, and then catching Mrs. Collins's gaze he walked up to her and whispered in her ear. Smiling at him, Charlotte stood and walked towards Anne.

"I believe you need some company, Miss De Bourgh," she said pleasantly, accepting the chair Fitzwilliam quickly obtained for her.

"Am I taking you away from your friends?" Anne asked.

"Not at all. My conversation isn't required in a group of chatterboxes," Charlotte said diplomatically. Anyone looking at the group would fail to see many interactions taking place. It seemed that Lady Catherine was, as usual, holding court with the occasional comment from Sir James.

"In that case, I shall welcome your company," Anne said quietly.

Fitzwilliam and Prudence left the pair, Charlotte encouraging Anne to speak, whilst the dancing couple took their place in the long-ways set.

"I could not utter the words properly when at Rosings, but I must say you look beautiful tonight, Cousin," Fitzwilliam said as they met across the set.

"You flatter me, Fitzwilliam. I've never had the word beautiful associated with my looks. A long Meg, or a robust woman, perhaps," Prudence responded.

"I will not have it that those are the best compliments you've ever received," Fitzwilliam said.

"You forget, I am a worker bee. We are far more focused on making a profit than wasting time on boosting one's self-esteem."

"Is there not time for both?"

"When Papa meets with his fellow friends, they talk business rather than pleasure. Development in the city is moving so fast there seems no time for changes to be implemented before the next one is being talked about. Perhaps we do not wish to waste a moment."

"I've never considered it a waste of time, flirting with someone I like."

"Is that what we're doing?" Prudence asked in surprise, but although the words were unexpected, a trickle of pleasure ran through her body.

"I'd certainly like it to be. Unfortunately, you seem to be determined on a more pragmatic conversation," Fitzwilliam smiled.

"I would not know how to start to flirt with someone," Prudence admitted.

"Would you be willing to learn?"

Prudence flushed. "Yes. I think I would."

Fitzwilliam raised her hand to his lips and quickly dropped a kiss onto her gloved hand. "Good. I was hoping you'd be agreeable. I am beginning to realise this might be the best visit I have ever made to Rosings."

It was a good thing they were separated from each other in the dance because the ever-practical Prudence needed a moment to gather her thoughts. She smiled blandly at the gentleman from the next couple as he turned her in the dance sequence, but she wasn't concentrating on him.

Fitzwilliam wanted to flirt with her. Was it a serious flirtation or just one to pass a visit that he had to endure rather than enjoy? She knew he was looking for an heiress, but he hadn't seemed to be bothered about her background, or the little she'd told him of it.

Shaking herself inwardly, she sighed. Of course he was just funning with her. He had been clear on the type of woman he wished to marry. He didn't consider her eligible. Why had her mind immediately raced to thoughts of marriage? She wasn't usually so fanciful. She should just enjoy a flirtation for what it was and then forget him when his visit came to an end.

A pity then that since the moment she'd met him, she had thought of little else.

After their second dance, Fitzwilliam accompanied her into the refreshment room and obtained two glasses of lemonade for them.

"It's as bad as attending a dance at Almack's," he grimaced as he drank the lemonade.

"Not a place to be rowdily drunk?" Prudence asked with a smile.

"No. The list of rules is longer than my arm, yet people are desperate to get an invite to it. Never really seen the attraction myself," Fitzwilliam admitted. "People too full of their own importance for my liking."

"You are a simple soul?"

"Yes. Being at war teaches you to enjoy the small things in life. When in Europe, a bed under cover was a luxury, or a bottle of wine bought or bartered from the locals was exquisite," Fitzwilliam admitted.

"True. A day out in the countryside, breathing fresh air and no smog is a delightful way to spend a day for factory workers," Prudence said. "Something the people of Kent would take for granted."

Fitzwilliam gave her a sideways look. "Is life very hard?"

"It can be," Prudence admitted. "It's hard work and long hours, but some of the mill owners are good men and do not mind spending a little of their profit on the welfare of their staff. Not all mind."

"And your employer?"

Prudence seemed to be on the verge of saying something and then changed her mind. "Mine is of the benevolent kind," she answered.

"Good."

"I must say, Cousin, you aren't doing well in the flirtation stakes. This is a very serious conversation for a ballroom," Prudence said with a laugh, changing the subject onto safer topics.

"I am losing my touch!" Fitzwilliam responded equally as lightly. "Come, I shall return you to our cousin, but I promise a better performance in the future."

Returning to Anne, Prudence smiled on seeing Mr. Huxley talking to Anne and Charlotte. It seemed her reserved cousin was gaining a little courage, for although she was blushing beetroot red, she was answering Mr. Huxley with a smile and was animated when speaking.

Miss Goode had also returned from dancing and was talking to Charlotte. Fitzwilliam and Prudence both headed towards Charlotte, rather than Anne, each not wishing to disturb their cousin.

After introductions and niceties had been exchanged, Fitzwilliam secured Miss Goode, and they went to join the next dance. Prudence watched their progression in the cotillion with a surprising amount of envy. Miss Goode was very pretty and could clearly flirt far easier than Prudence if Fitzwilliam's laughter were anything to go by.

"Miss Goode was telling me she's just returned from a school in Switzerland. She seems very well travelled," Charlotte said.

"Pretty and educated. A perfect combination," Prudence said, glad her voice didn't sound bitter. She couldn't be so uncharitable against a fellow female.

"And with a healthy dowry. Sir James is convinced she will secure a fine match on her first season. They delayed her come out because she wanted to see some of the world before settling down," Charlotte continued.

"I don't blame her. Going from the schoolroom to a marriage seems very strange. One can have little life experience."

"Sometimes that would be of benefit to both the husband and wife," Charlotte responded with a smile. "Although in Miss Goode's respect, that will not be the case."

"I would imagine she'll have suitors fighting over her."

"Yes. Although Colonel Fitzwilliam could probably fix her attention if he put his mind to it, if their first meeting is any indication of how well they will get on."

"You can't plan a life on the basis of a first meeting!" Prudence exclaimed.

"Perhaps not, but Colonel Fitzwilliam isn't getting any younger. He needs to make a short courtship if he wishes to secure someone like Miss Goode. Once they have reached London, there will be beaux aplenty to turn her head. He might not fare so well there."

"If an attachment develops on both their parts, I'm sure a trip to London will not alter their affections. It wouldn't for me."

"Not with someone in reduced circumstances like Colonel Fitzwilliam, but for Miss Goode, she will have the pick of the *ton*," Charlotte answered authoritatively.

"How depressingly fickle," Prudence said.

Chapter 6

A knock on her bedchamber door stopped Prudence from becoming depressed from what she'd heard that evening. She couldn't curse anyone but herself for how the evening had turned out. True, Fitzwilliam had returned to their group and danced with Charlotte and then escorted Anne and Lady Catherine into supper, but she couldn't shake off the feeling that he'd been smitten with Miss Goode. He would not neglect his duties to his family no matter how delighted he was with the young girl.

Acknowledging the knock, she wasn't surprised when Anne entered the room, all flushed cheeks and sparkling eyes. Prudence smiled at her cousin.

"Did you see how attentive he was?" Anne asked, sitting on the edge of the chaise longue.

"I take it we are discussing Sir James towards Lady Catherine?"

"Don't be cruel!" Anne chastised.

Prudence laughed. "Of course, I saw how attentive he was," she said. "Our cousin thinks Aunt Catherine would never countenance a match between you. Be careful, Anne. Flirt with him, but do not have your heart broken by your mother's wishes."

Anne's smile slipped. "I know it is futile. But I do so like him. He is the only man who doesn't frighten me, apart from Fitzwilliam of course. But he is different."

"Your mother would never consider a marriage between you and Fitzwilliam? It surprises me somewhat that she is not encouraging a match between you two. She wanted you to marry Cousin Darcy after all," Prudence couldn't resist saying, although depending on the answer, she could be torturing herself even further than she had since she had met Miss Goode.

"Oh, no! Fitzwilliam is not important enough for mother to give her approval. I'm relieved to say that I would wish a marriage to him as little as one to Darcy, but for different reasons," Anne said.

"You seem to be on easy terms with Fitzwilliam."

"We are, but he would find life very dull with me. I enjoy the quiet life. Fitzwilliam is a man who is always doing something. I pity him when he is here, for he is like a caged animal," Anne revealed.

"I suppose it comes down to his military career."

"Possibly. He needs an active life with someone who can challenge him. For, although he is the second son, he's so charming he is very often spoiled and fussed over."

"And does he realise this is how you see him?"

"No. As you say, I have claws, but they are well-hidden," Anne grinned at Prudence.

"Anne, you are definitely my favourite family member," Prudence responded, pushing aside her inner voice, which accused her of lying as she uttered the words, for that title belonged to a cousin with laughing green eyes and an easy smile.

*

Anne felt too tired to venture out of doors the morning after the assembly, so Prudence rode out instead of using the gig.

Galloping over the fields belonging to the Rosings estate, she let her hat fall onto her back and her hair stream behind her in a tangle of knotted curls. Windswept and exuberant, she brought the horse to a stop and turned it to look back over the hill she had ridden over.

Seeing a rider following her, she smiled. He looked very well on a horse, as if he'd been born to it, which he probably had.

She waited until he caught up, his ready smile on his lips.

"Cousin! I thought I would never catch you," Fitzwilliam admitted.

"I had an urge to see the view."

Turning reluctantly to look behind him, Fitzwilliam moved until he was close to Prudence. "Looking at you is preferable even to the rolling hills of Kent."

"Are we flirting again?" Prudence asked.

"When you look so fine, it is inevitable," Fitzwilliam answered.

"I look like the hoyden my aunt accused me of being and grieve the brushing of my tangled locks that I shall have to endure to make myself presentable for visits later today."

An image of brushing her hair for her made Fitzwilliam turn away from Prudence for a moment whilst he gathered himself. He didn't know what was happening to him with regards to his feelings towards her. It was bad enough that he sought out her company at every possible opportunity, but now he was imagining instances that he'd never imagined with anyone else he had ever met. It was disturbing.

When his emotions were under control once more, he turned to look at Prudence. He smiled wistfully. She looked beautiful. Windswept, with colour in her cheeks and an exquisitely fitted riding habit made her look like just the type of woman he could feel proud to have at his side.

His jaw clenched. He was being a fool. He couldn't afford to let her get under his skin. He had to marry for money. A pity it seemed a very cold way of looking at wedded bliss when he was so near Prudence. That was also a new sensation. He'd never felt so bereft at being unable to choose his own bride as he had these last few days.

"You seem troubled, Cousin," Prudence said, having watched Fitzwilliam with interest.

"I am just concerned that it will be weeks before we will dance again. That is if we can persuade Aunt Catherine to indulge us a second time."

"Oh, I think she enjoyed the venture overall," Prudence said. "Everyone was suitably deferential towards her, and those beneath her touch did not approach her at all, showing their good sense."

"You really have our aunt worked out, don't you? You are obviously a discerning person."

"She is not a complex character," Prudence shrugged. "I admit she can be frustrating, but as I am hardly likely to be spending much time with her over the years, her idiosyncrasies will not cause me any loss of sleep."

"Are you thinking of leaving us already?" Fitzwilliam asked in sudden panic.

"No. But I cannot remain here forever. I have never been so idle in my life."

"Nor I," Fitzwilliam admitted. "But I am finding that I am enjoying my time on this visit. I was only to come for a week in the first instance, but I have been delaying my departure."

Prudence tried to control her elation at the words. It could be because he was interested in Miss Goode, she cursed herself. How foolish would she seem if that were the case? Her thoughts did not stop her hoping that it was herself who was delaying his departure.

"If that is so, I think we should take every opportunity to find out who is best on horseback," she said.

"You do know I spent months travelling on my horse through Spain, Portugal, and France, don't you?" Fitzwilliam answered with his winning grin.

"In that case, a head start is not unreasonable," Prudence said, digging her horse with her heels and setting off at a gallop. She heard Fitzwilliam's laugh behind her but didn't turn. Hunkering down over the neck of her horse, she urged him on.

Fitzwilliam followed, and although he caught up, Prudence was no novice at horse riding. She was challenging his abilities even though he was confident of winning in the end. Instead he chose to lull her into a false sense of security.

Racing towards the house, Fitzwilliam decided it was time to show his prowess. Urging his steed for a final push, he began to overtake Prudence.

Laughing at the curse she aimed in his direction, he continued to make progress, clattering along the gravel path and around the corner into the stable yard. Coming to an abrupt halt, he leapt from his horse, landing nimbly and stood, arms folded, leaning on the door post of the stable building.

Prudence was moments behind him, and bringing her horse to a stop, she couldn't contain her laughter. "You cad! That's not very gentlemanly of you!" She accepted his help in dismounting and slid into his arms as he lifted her from her mount.

"You laid the rules down by cheating at the start," Fitzwilliam smiled down at her, keeping his grasp around her waist.

Prudence hit his shoulder with her hastily removed gloves. "It's only a rogue who would point out that a lady tried to gain the upper hand, for all the good it did me."

"Never put yourself up against a cavalry officer in a horse race. You made the fatal error of underestimating your rival."

"Lesson learned, believe me!"

There was a pause between them, as if each were waiting for the other to do or say something. Fitzwilliam moved his head slightly, lowering it towards Prudence, but then a groom began to move her horse, and the pair, realising they were in a busy stable yard, pulled themselves apart.

"I had better get inside and make myself decent," Prudence said quietly.

"I will make sure the horses are tended to before I come in."

"Thank you."

Prudence stepped away, but Fitzwilliam grabbed her hand and brought it to his lips. "You still look beautiful."

Eyes widening at his actions as much as his words, Prudence flushed. Unable to think of a suitable retort, she gave a swift curtsy and walked away towards the house and her chamber.

Fitzwilliam watched her retreat, not knowing whether he should chase after her to kiss her, apologise for his rakish behaviour, or beg for her hand in marriage. He shook himself. What was he thinking? Marriage? He had never wanted to marry anyone he'd ever met, yet here he was considering marrying Prudence?

Striding into the stable, he shrugged his shoulders. He had allowed himself to have his head turned by a pretty face. That was all. He would soon come to his senses. He needed to marry for money.

She was utterly charming though. Funny and challenging. And sweet.

Oh, dear Lord!

*

Prudence took her time making herself presentable. She hadn't brought a maid with her, and Lady Catherine hadn't assigned anyone to attend her, just letting one of the housemaids assist her when necessary. Thankfully, for the assembly, Anne had insisted her own ladies' maid should help them both.

She looked ruefully at her reflection in the looking glass. She was playing with fire; she knew that. Papa had insisted she go without announcing the reality of her home situation. He wanted her to receive a genuine welcome for herself and not what material things she brought with her.

It had seemed so straight forward when in her father's drawing room, but now it wasn't so clear-cut. She was deceiving Fitzwilliam and Anne, and that didn't rest easy with her.

She could admit the truth of her situation, and then Fitzwilliam might consider marrying her. No. She didn't want that. Actually, a part of her did want exactly that, but whoever married her had to do so because of herself, not the money she brought to the marriage.

Who was she trying to fool? He would be as likely to attach himself to her — a daughter of a 'cit' — as he would a poor-as-a-church-mouse spinster! She was being foolhardy in thinking he would want anything but a mild flirtation with her. He was a member of the *ton*. They socialised in their own circles. Marrying her would mean leaving his society behind, and he would never do that.

She blew out her cheeks. There she was again, thinking of marriage. She had never thought so much of that state until she'd met Fitzwilliam, and now she could think of little else.

Anne had already said Fitzwilliam was bored to death when at Rosings. Prudence would just have to accept that she was providing a little interest or entertainment. A pity her heart ached at the thought, but she was sensible and could drag herself out of her melancholy even if it took a lot of inward scolding on her part.

Chapter 7

Sir James, his mother, and his unmarried daughter all paid a visit to Rosings to offer an invitation to the party.

"We wish to hold an evening's entertainment in honour of Miss De Bourgh," he said with a deferential nod towards Lady Catherine. "It has been too long since our company have seen her, and she is looking very well."

"I am not sure another night out so soon would be of benefit to Anne's constitution." Lady Catherine's quick response dashed the hopes of the others in the room.

"Oh, Mama, if I rest during the day like I did for the assembly, I'm sure I will be fine. Sir James's house is hardly half the distance of Westerham," Anne said, astounding everyone in the room, but especially her mother.

Lady Catherine narrowed her eyes towards Prudence, silently accusing her of Anne's disobedience, but Prudence just returned the accusatory stare with a bland expression.

Sir James thought it advisable to intervene in the suddenly tense atmosphere. "I shall ensure that every consideration for Miss De Bourgh's comfort is taken into account, and only a few of the more suitable members of the locality will be invited," he assured Lady Catherine. "It would be such a pity if you were to miss out on advising us of what decoration we should choose when we refurbish the drawing room. I was saying to you only yesterday — wasn't I

Mother? — that we needed to seek Lady Catherine's advice."

Uttering the perfect words to ensure Lady Catherine would respond in the positive made everyone in the room glad of Sir James's diplomacy skills.

"I will certainly advise you what to do with regards to decoration," Lady Catherine said. "Mrs. Morton said only a few days ago what a help I'd been with regards to her dining room. The extra expense of the Chinese wallpaper was worth it, she said. She had never seen a room look so grand."

"Precisely," Sir James said. "Which is why we seek the advice of such an informed person as yourself."

"We shall arrive at four, but we can stay no longer than eleven," Lady Catherine instructed.

"May we have a little dancing, Papa?" Miss Goode asked, looking shyly at Colonel Fitzwilliam.

"We shall see on the day. We would not want to plan anything that would spoil Miss De Bourgh's enjoyment."

"Anne will not be dancing, but Prudence can play the piano for those who wish to do so," Lady Catherine said.

"I do not play an instrument as well as other young ladies do, Aunt," Prudence said quickly. She spoke the truth, but she also didn't want to spend the whole night at the piano.

"You have a week to practice, then," Lady Catherine responded damningly.

Prudence sagged. It seemed her evening was to end with sore fingers and no opportunity to dance!

The three cousins remained in the morning room when the guests left, while Lady Catherine followed Sir

James and his family to the door, issuing instructions as she went.

Prudence smiled at her cousin. "You stood up to your mother. I was most impressed."

Anne blushed. "I couldn't resist speaking out. It was such a nice thing for Sir James to do — to arrange a party in my honour."

"I think he has two motives," Prudence said, looking archly at Fitzwilliam who was sitting near the two women.

"Oh?" he asked in response.

"I think they want to see more of Anne, which I'm not surprised at and can only like the family all the more for it, but I also think that a certain Colonel is an appealing suitor for Miss Goode," Prudence said.

Fitzwilliam laughed. "She will be set for someone far more important than I!"

"Oh, I don't know. She does look at you a great deal," Anne interjected.

"Does she? And are my two cousins very jealous at the thought of my running off with Miss Goode?" Fitzwilliam asked with arched eyebrows.

"We're devastated," Prudence responded in the same tone in which the question had been asked. "Aren't we Anne? To the point that I shall practice the pianoforte every day to ensure you have perfectly played dances in which to flirt."

Fitzwilliam pulled a face. "That was poorly done by our aunt. It is Sir James's responsibility to sort out a person to provide the music, not Aunt Catherine's."

"I think it was my punishment for her suspecting I was the person behind Anne standing up to her," Prudence admitted.

"Oh, no! Surely not!" Anne said, hurriedly. "I will speak to mother, if that is the case."

"I wouldn't," Fitzwilliam said quickly. "That would almost surely convince her of the fact."

"Dealing with mother can be so difficult," Anne said with a frown.

Prudence smiled at her cousin. "You are getting better at it."

"Shall we escape to the gardens for a walk before she comes back?" Fitzwilliam offered.

"I should not. I do not think mother would approve," Anne said.

"I shall pass on your regards to Mr. Huxley, if we pass him," Prudence said.

"I'll return with my pelisse in a moment," Anne said, hurrying out of the room.

"You are playing with fire, Cousin," Fitzwilliam warned.

"I've already spoken to Anne about guarding her heart," Prudence said. "But she needs to spend more time outside whilst the weather is mild. She looks a lot better since I arrived and we started our daily constitutionals. She was a feeble little thing. I was quite taken aback at the state of her."

"Yes, you have had a positive influence on her. I hope it continues when you have had enough of us. For I know you will abandon us at some point."

"Oh, I cannot see that happening just yet," Prudence smiled at him.

*

The threesome walked along the pathways in the terraced garden. None of them wanted to wear out Anne and suffer the wrath of Lady Catherine.

"Shall we spend a day in Westerham shopping before our visit to Sir James's?" Prudence asked.

"I'm afraid not," Anne said regretfully. "Mother would never agree to it. And to be fair, it would be a little tiring."

"In that case, I shall not mention it again," Prudence said quickly.

"Could I get you what you need?" Fitzwilliam offered.

"It would do me a real service if you would accompany me," Prudence said. "I would rather play the music I'm used to, and I'm afraid Lady Catherine does not have the music sheets for it. I'm sure I could find what I need in Westerham."

"I shall happily escort you. Shall we travel on horseback?"

"And give you the chance of leaving me standing again? No thank you, sir! I shall insist we ride in the gig, and I can ridicule your handling of the horses," Prudence laughed.

"You will be disappointed. Again," Fitzwilliam warned.

"Prudence is a fine horsewoman," Anne defended her cousin. "You are trying to show off, Fitzwilliam. Be careful, or you will come unstuck."

"Two of you against me! Well, I'll be dashed. If this carries on I'll need to send out for reinforcements."

"We are hardly a match for a gentleman of the highest calibre. Perhaps you have fooled us into feeling sorry for you when you just wish to lull us into a false sense of security," Prudence said airily.

"Why would I want to do that?" Fitzwilliam asked.

"So that when you stand up to us or Aunt Catherine, it would shock us and her into letting you do as you please. I'm quite suspicious at how amenable you seemed when you twisted our aunt into doing just as you wished for the ball."

"Darcy always made sure Fitzwilliam was with him because he wanted someone who could make pretty to Mama. Darcy never could," Anne said candidly.

Fitzwilliam looked at his cousin in astonishment, but Prudence let out a crack of laughter.

"What is it, Fitzwilliam?" she asked, still chuckling. "Seeing the real Anne for the first time?"

"Why, I do believe I am," Fitzwilliam answered with a rueful smile.

"I'm usually very quiet," Anne explained. "Most people forget that I'm there."

"I shan't be doing that in future!" Fitzwilliam said. "In fact, I cannot wait to tell Darcy of this more spirited Anne. He will be astounded."

"Oh, do not!" Anne appealed. "I should be mortified."

"Don't take on so, dearest Anne," Prudence soothed. "He is funning with you, and we should punish him for it."

"How could we do that?"

"We could spread the rumour that he's considering a career in the clergy now that the dastardly Napoleon has been defeated. I am sure Mr. Collins would be happy to give him more than a little advice in his choice of career," Prudence said.

"You wouldn't," Fitzwilliam said, choking.

"Is that a dare, sir?"

"Good God, no! I'm not that bumbleheaded! I shall beg forgiveness and promise not to write to Darcy," he assured Anne.

Anne smiled around Fitzwilliam to glance at Prudence. "Thank you."

"It is my pleasure, and you'll always be safe in the knowledge that you now know our cousin's Achilles' heel."

"Termagant."

"Oh, most certainly," Prudence replied.

Chapter 8

Lady Catherine suddenly required a list of supplies so long that Fitzwilliam half regretted offering to accompany his cousin. Such thoughts were banished the moment Prudence came down the stairs, resplendent in a green riding habit with gold braiding.

Pulling on her gold gloves, she smiled at him. "Are you ready to take the reins, Cousin?"

"If it means I get to spend most of the day with the fine creature before me, I am ready, indeed!" Fitzwilliam said with a bow and an offer of his arm.

Prudence flushed at the compliment but laughed it off. "You are ridiculous. Come, we shall be lucky to return before nightfall with all the commissions Aunt Catherine has set you."

They rode at a brisk pace, Fitzwilliam as capable in a gig as he was on horseback. Prudence could admire her protector whilst they were barrelling along, chatting amiably.

He was so easy to like, she cursed inwardly. Charming, and although not as handsome as some men she'd met, he certainly had an air about him that was very appealing. When he smiled and his eyes twinkled at her as they often did, she felt the gesture to the tips of her fingers. More than once, she had to restrain herself from her fingers reaching out to him. Such forward behaviour would never do. He might be easy-going, but he belonged to a society that condemned anything that went against the strict rules of etiquette.

Arriving in Westerham, Fitzwilliam decided they would get the music sheets first. "I would not wish you to be in a panic if it should look as if we might run out of time."

Prudence gave him a sideways glance. "Can you honestly see me becoming distracted over such an inconsequential thing? You must think women feeble creatures if you can."

Fitzwilliam smiled. "No. I actually think you very capable, but there are many who would develop a fit of the vapours over such a trifle."

"Goodness me, there are many things I'm thankful for, one being I wasn't introduced to society."

"Why would you say that?"

"I doubt I would be well received for slapping the face of anyone so insipid as to react in such a way," Prudence responded. "What milksops do you surround yourself with?"

"Oh, there are many, believe me," Fitzwilliam said with meaning in his tone.

"What a sorry state of affairs. You are more likely to get into a quake if you don't finish Aunt Catherine's shopping, than I will."

"You will not get any argument from me about that!" Fitzwilliam responded.

They spent the next few hours in easy companionship as they walked the length and breadth of the main shopping street, which surrounded a pretty green. It was a busy small town, supplying many of the villages surrounding it, which made it a vibrant place.

When they finished shopping, Fitzwilliam insisted they stop at one of the Black Eagle Brewery Inns and secure a private room in which to refresh themselves.

"They brew a fine ale. Darcy and myself have been coming here for years," Fitzwilliam assured her, taking off his hat and gloves. Laying his greatcoat over a chair, he walked to the fire. "It is mild for the time of year, but the cold eventually seeps in. Come near the fire, Cousin. I shan't be letting you get chilled as I did in the garden."

Prudence did as she was bid. She had taken off her bonnet and gloves, welcoming the warmth of the fire. "We should make haste to return, for the night will close in on us."

"It will, but I shall hire us a coach. I should have thought it through before we set out. It will be too chilly, returning in the gig. I will collect it tomorrow."

"I hope you travel early. I would not wish Anne to miss her morning trip out."

"You're a hard task master. I am only usually below stairs so early at Rosings because of the early hours Aunt Catherine keeps. You'd have me rising with the lark!"

"It is character building. Where I come from, the knocker upper would make sure you rose at the appointed time."

"Even the name sends me into shudders," Fitzwilliam responded.

"You poor, spoilt boy," Prudence laughed. "I would like to see you work in a mill for a week. You'd be eaten alive."

"No doubt." Fitzwilliam smiled. "Although you've survived and are still a genteel lady." There was so much about Prudence that didn't quite add up in Fitzwilliam's mind.

"I have had advantages that most workers do not have," Prudence admitted.

"One is the quality of your clothes. You always look exquisite," Fitzwilliam said.

Blushing, Prudence smiled. "My mother had good taste and only went to the finest people when she needed clothing. I suppose it was what she'd been used to, and Papa always liked her looking her best. He has just transferred that wish onto me, so I benefit. There are some talented seamstresses in Manchester. Not everyone dresses in sackcloth."

"I would never have supposed it for a moment," Fitzwilliam defended himself.

"Aunt Catherine does."

"Thankfully, Aunt Catherine's views are about as far away from mine as is possible. I shall secure a carriage before we sit down to eat."

When Fitzwilliam left the room, Prudence cursed herself silently. She'd had the perfect opportunity to reveal herself to him. Why hadn't she? There was no need to tell him everything, just enough for him to realise that she had no need to take up a post her aunt had threatened to find for her. Instead, she'd taken the cowardly way out. Again.

Fitzwilliam soon came back, and the banter continued between the pair. When they were leaving the inn, Fitzwilliam offered his arm and helped Prudence into the carriage. He accepted two hot bricks and placed them at her feet.

"I insist you have one of these," Prudence said, using her booted foot to push one of the bricks towards Fitzwilliam. "I am not the type of female who will make others suffer whilst she sits in comfort."

"Thank you, but I don't know how you will deal with the fact that there's only one blanket to cover your knees," Fitzwilliam smiled at her.

"In that case, sit next to me, and we will share," Prudence said, wriggling sideways so there was room enough for him to join her on the seat.

Fitzwilliam didn't need to be asked twice. He moved seats and let Prudence fix the blanket across both their laps.

"There. We shall both be comfortable, and I won't feel guilty," Prudence said with a smile.

"I would be more comfortable if I did this," Fitzwilliam said, reaching out for her hand and bringing it to his lips.

Prudence eyed him. "And what have I done to warrant such a gesture?"

"Oh, you've been funny, beautiful, and lovely ever since my arrival at Rosings," Fitzwilliam admitted.

"Thank you, but I have to suggest your eyes are faulty and you are easily pleased."

Laughing, Fitzwilliam kissed her hand again. "You are a delight." The mood suddenly changed. It was as if they were back in the stable yard, but this time there was no one else around.

"If you are going to kiss me, Fitzwilliam, please do it now," Prudence said. "I would hate a sudden unexpected stop of the carriage to prevent it."

With a chuckle, Fitzwilliam pulled her to him, and not a moment too soon in both their opinions, kissed her soundly.

Her bonnet and his stove top hat landed on the floor. Arms wrapped around waists and necks, and Prudence was pulled onto Fitzwilliam's lap. Grabbing handfuls of his hair, she revelled in the feel of it, something she'd been wishing to do for days.

Fitzwilliam moaned at Prudence's actions but forced himself to pull away slightly. Cupping her face in his hands, he smiled into eyes that were wide and unfocused.

"I've wanted to do that for so long. I did not know what it was like to ache for someone, but I know now."

"I've felt the same," Prudence said quietly.

"May I continue to kiss you? I will stop if you want me to."

Prudence groaned and pulled him to her lips. Laughing and wrapping his arms around her waist once more, he quietly proceeded to make it the most enjoyable carriage ride either had ever shared.

If the coachman noticed slightly dishevelled passengers alighting from the carriage, it was nothing new to him. If the butler noticed the flushed cheeks of Colonel Fitzwilliam and Miss Prudence, he wouldn't mention it to any other member of staff, old romantic that he was.

As a result, both Fitzwilliam and Prudence reached their respective bedchambers, one flopping against the door, the other onto her bed, both experiencing jubilant but confusing emotions at their day out.

*

Walking through the long gallery the following morning, Prudence was grabbed from behind and swung around until she was facing Fitzwilliam.

"Good morning, beautiful," Fitzwilliam said, landing a kiss on her lips. "How are you this fine morning?"

Prudence laughed and snaked her arms around his neck. "All the better for seeing you. Although I should ask if you regularly accost young women when they least expect it?"

"Only the ones who fill my dreams with their kisses."

"Oh, Fitzwilliam, you do say the sweetest things," Prudence groaned.

"You say that as if it's a bad thing," Fitzwilliam answered, kissing her again.

Putting her hands on his chest to stay him, Prudence shook her head at him. "We cannot do this."

"Why not?"

"I'll be thrown out if we are discovered."

"I'll follow you."

"You are nonsensical sometimes," Prudence laughed at him.

"I want to experience as many of your kisses as possible. Is that wrong?"

"I'm no lightskirt," Prudence said, a little cruelly because she knew without doubt Fitzwilliam would not be so disrespectful towards her, but it had to be said.

Fitzwilliam stepped back. "Is that what you think I'm trying to do? Offer you a carte blanche?"

"I just wanted to make it clear that I'm not a woman of easy virtue. I have never kissed anyone before."

"What? Not even the most handsome man in the mill?" Fitzwilliam teased.

Prudence punched him in the arm. "Just because I'm unkissed does not mean I haven't been courted or offered marriage."

Her words immediately doused the humour in Fitzwilliam's expression. "Have you? By whom?"

Shaking her head at him, she asked, "Fitzwilliam, do you know how arrogant and presumptuous you've been?"

"No. I—"

"Yes. You have," Prudence interrupted. "It's a good thing I like you, for I could box your ears. I really could."

"Sorry. But it is not my fault. Truly."

"And whose fault is it, pray tell?"

"Yours."

"Mine?" Prudence spluttered.

"Yesterday, I admitted that I ached for you, which I've never done with anyone else. I would just like to reiterate that, and today you've made me as jealous as a young fop with his first infatuation," Fitzwilliam admitted.

"You are truly ridiculous."

"But loveable with it?"

"Perhaps a little."

"That will do for me." Fitzwilliam didn't wait for any further response; he took Prudence in his arms once more and showed her, without words, just how loveable he could be.

When they eventually separated, both were flushed and breathless.

"This must stop," Prudence said. "And this time I am being serious."

"Why?"

"What happens if we are caught, Fitzwilliam? Can you see yourself living in Manchester with me? For I promise you this, I won't ever live in London," Prudence said. "Do you want to risk compromising me if that is the consequence?"

Fitzwilliam paled. He had been playing a dangerous game. They were still strangers really, and Prudence could demand he marry her. He hadn't been thinking sensibly, just reacting to her. He should have thought of the consequences earlier. He was a fool. "I suppose I already have compromised you."

"Don't be silly. We have both enjoyed the kisses. They were something we both wanted. But I cannot risk any further foolishness. I won't bring any shame onto my father. He is most precious to me," Prudence explained reluctantly.

"Of course not. I am sorry, Prudence. I acted the cad."

"That is the first time you've ever used my given name." Prudence smiled, lightening the mood. "Come. We can put it down to a pleasurable experience, a moment of madness. But we shall still be the best of friends, won't we?"

"You will be a most treasured one to me," Fitzwilliam said honestly.

"Good. We can go on as we were before," Prudence said, but there was a little less light in her eyes than normal. It went unnoticed by the man who was in as much turmoil as she.

*

Almost a week passed before it was the evening of the party held at Sir James' house. Evenings had been trying for both Fitzwilliam and Prudence. Paranoid that their behaviour was being watched, for there was little that Lady Catherine failed to notice, they were on guard as to how they behaved with each other. As a result, their interactions were stilted and awkward.

Even Anne had looked at them frowningly on a number of occasions. It was driving them both mad.

Prudence took longer than usual to get ready for the party. She did not want to go. How could she stand to watch Fitzwilliam flirt and dance with Miss Goode when she had been the one to push him away? She could have had a week of kisses. But no, she had to be sensible and honourable, and it would go down as one of the biggest regrets of her life.

Pinning the fall front of her dress in place, she smiled to herself. At least she would be dressed in the height of fashion; Papa had made sure of that. Picking up her sapphires that would enhance the ice blue satin of her dress, she looked well enough. Not beautiful, no matter that Fitzwilliam tried to convince her of it, but she loved him for it.

Love.

One small word that meant so much. She truly loved him, and looking at herself in the mirror, she decided this was ridiculous. She held their future in her own hands. If she were truthful, they could go on without restraint. Yes. That was it. She would confess all tomorrow.

Fitzwilliam waited in the drawing room for the ladies in the party. Swirling a brandy in the large bulbous glass he was holding, he realised something that had been niggling at him for days. He wanted to marry her. He'd never wished to wed anyone else he had ever met, but he wanted Prudence. That was all well and good. He congratulated himself on choosing the finest woman in the land. There was one problem. Money.

Knocking back the liquid in one fell swoop, he silently cursed. It always came down to money.

Anne entered the room dressed in a pale gold dress, which suited her colouring perfectly. She smiled shyly at her cousin.

"You look beautiful, my dear," Fitzwilliam said gently. "I wish you could have a season in London."

"I would not enjoy it," Anne admitted. "I'm not as strong as Prudence. I would wilt under the round of entertainments and the gossip and censure if I made a mistake."

"Perhaps. It can be hard. Although you are wrong about our cousin. She has admitted she wouldn't live in London."

"She's strong and able. I think perhaps she might at some point change her mind. For the right person, of course," Anne said, with a nervous glance at her cousin.

"Are we that obvious?" Fitzwilliam asked. There was no point in pretending with Anne. She'd spent too much time with them not to have noticed some affection between them.

"A little."

"It's a useless cause, Anne. I cannot marry her, for I want to provide a good living for my future family."

"Is there nothing you can do? Appeal to my mother? I do not mind giving you some of my inheritance, for I'm hardly likely to spend it all," Anne offered.

Walking over to his cousin, he grasped her by the hands and kissed her on the cheek. "Thank you, Anne, for your kind offer. It isn't possible, but I am eternally grateful that you would be good enough to make such a kind gesture."

Anne blushed. "It's partially selfish on my part. If I gave away some of my fortune, I might be able to not be so far above the person I like."

"We are a fine pair, are we not?" Fitzwilliam groaned. "What a hash we are making of our lives. I will tell you this. When I finally give up hope of finding an heiress to fool into marrying me, I shall return to Rosings and live off you for the rest of my days. We shall have each other for company."

Laughing, Anne turned as the door opened. "Be careful what you wish for, Cousin, I might hold you to that."

Prudence entered the room with Lady Catherine and was gratified at the expression on Fitzwilliam's face as he took in her dress, which was sliding over her figure in a most tantalising way. He swallowed before making his bow to his aunt, reluctantly tearing his eyes away from Prudence.

The three made their way to the party. Once again, Lady Catherine had condescended to convey the Collins's to the Goode family. Mr. Collins kept the conversation flowing whilst the others in the carriage took solace in their own thoughts.

Thirty people made up the party at Sir James's house. He was an amenable host, welcoming and hospitable without being overbearing.

Prudence spoke a little to every member of the family and decided that, putting aside her jealousy of Miss Goode, the whole family were thoroughly decent people. She perhaps was more inclined to find pleasure now that she had decided to take control of her life and be honest with the man she'd fallen in love with. Yes, life was proving to be very good indeed.

Before the dancing started, some of the young ladies present had the opportunity of showing off their abilities on the pianoforte. When Prudence was entreated to play, Fitzwilliam surprised her by offering his hand.

"Let us perform a duet, Cousin," he said with his ready smile.

"Really?" Prudence squeaked. "I accepted I'd have to play, but there was no mention of singing!"

"Don't worry. My voice will carry for us both if yours is so awful."

"Beast," she muttered, but a laugh gurgled, and she approached the instrument with a ready smile on her face.

If anyone watching the pair had any doubt in their mind about the affection each held for the other, by the end of the love song they performed, no one was under any illusion that there was going to be some sort of announcement in the not too distant future.

Lady Catherine looked livid, but remained poised and her usual self during the night. Even when Mr. and Mrs. Collins had been set down at the parsonage, she remained silent.

On entering Rosings, she announced to the group. "We shall have an extra at luncheon tomorrow. I expect us all to dine at one. I expect you all to gather promptly." Without further explanation, she regally climbed the stairs, leaving the three standing in the hallway, equally puzzled.

"That sounds very mysterious," Fitzwilliam said. "Has she given you no clue to who is joining us, Anne?"

"Not at all. I cannot think who it could be," Anne admitted. "There's no point in trying to find out more. Mother obviously wants it to be a surprise. I shall say my goodnight to you both."

Prudence waited until Anne was halfway up the stairs before turning to Fitzwilliam. "I don't expect you to rise early, but could I have a moment to speak with you after luncheon? I have something I'd like to discuss with you to both our benefit."

"That sounds intriguing. Can we not speak of it now?"

"Better to do so when we are both clear-headed, I think," Prudence said. "Goodnight, Fitzwilliam. Thank you for tonight. It was a pleasure performing a duet with you."

"Your singing wasn't too bad after all," Fitzwilliam said with a grin. "I only had to increase the volume of my voice a time or two."

"You really are a rascal."

Chapter 9

The three cousins were dutifully seated in the dining room at Rosings Park by ten minutes to the hour. None of them wished to incur Lady Catherine's wrath by being late.

The said lady walked grandly into the room, her large embroidered day coat billowing out in its usual intimidating way. Her entrance made the three of them sit up straighter in anticipation of what was about to unfold.

They didn't have to wait long. In Lady Catherine's wake followed Mr. Darcy, tall and resplendent in his dark coat and buff coloured breeches.

"Darcy? What the devil are you doing here?" Fitzwilliam asked, standing to greet his cousin. "Is Elizabeth well?"

"Perfectly well, I thank you," Darcy responded shaking Fitzwilliam's hand.

"But I thought you did not wish to travel?"

"No. I didn't, but I received an express from Aunt Catherine," Darcy explained. "We'll speak later."

Fitzwilliam returned to the dining table, a frown on his usually smooth features. Darcy walked over to Prudence, and offered a bow.

"Miss Bamber, I am glad to finally make your acquaintance."

"And I you." Prudence responded, but her tone was cooler than normal.

Darcy greeted Anne before taking his seat at the dining table. There was no opportunity for the cousins to find out more about the visit as Lady Catherine dominated the conversation as she was wont to do.

After they'd finished their repast, Darcey asked Fitzwilliam to join him in the study. Lady Catherine looked on in approval as the two men made their bows to the ladies and left the room.

"Darcy is such a sensible man, his only fault was to marry that woman," Lady Catherine said of her favourite nephew.

"They both seem very happy," Anne responded in defence of her cousin-in-law.

"And how, pray, do you know this?" Lady Catherine demanded of her daughter.

"Mrs. Collins sometimes mentions Mrs. Darcy when she's received a letter from her," Anne said, blushing deep red at her mother's sharp question.

"I shall be telling Mrs. Collins what I think of her spreading the news from her private correspondence. She should have distanced herself from Miss Bennet by now," Lady Catherine said, unable to give Mrs. Darcy her married name.

"I presume Mrs. Collins feels herself to be fortunate that Mrs. Darcy still writes to her. A woman of such high status does not always remain in touch with those who are very much lower in the social scale," Prudence said, her anger prickling in defence of a cousin she'd never met.

Lady Catherine narrowed her eyes at her niece. "One has to know who it is acceptable to associate oneself with. There is nothing worse than a person thinking they are high in the instep when they should know their place."

Perceiving that the comment was aimed at herself more than the absent Mrs. Darcy, Prudence stood. "Please excuse me, Aunt. I have the urge to take a walk in the gardens."

"I'll join you," Anne said.

"It is too inclement for you, Anne," Lady Catherine interjected.

"I'll wrap up warm. I am accompanying Prudence," Anne said, defying her mother for the first time in her life.

Both ladies walked out of the dining room, leaving behind a fulminating Lady Catherine.

*

Darcy had used the study regularly over the years when undertaking duties to help his aunt. Although she was more than capable of dealing with her own business, occasionally she had requested the help of her nephew.

He walked into the room and poured two glasses of brandy from the decanter.

"What is the meaning of your visit, Darcy?" Fitzwilliam asked. "I had thought you to be reluctant to leave your wife at this delicate time."

"I am, but as I said, I received an express from Lady Catherine. I thought it pertinent to travel here, but I am keen to return to Pemberley. I hope to leave here tomorrow."

"What could she want that I could not have sorted out for her? It does not do my pride an ounce of good to know that I am on hand yet she didn't confide her troubles to me."

"I think you'll understand why when I explain the situation to you."

"In that case, explain away," Fitzwilliam said, but he was on the alert. His instincts were warning him that he was not going to be happy with what Darcy was going to say.

Darcy decided to come straight to the point. The cousins had shared many problems over the years and had always been honest and upfront with each other.

"Aunt Catherine is concerned that you are about to make a mésalliance," he admitted.

"What?" Fitzwilliam responded heatedly.

"That you have become besotted with Miss Bamber and are about to act rashly."

Fitzwilliam slammed down the glass onto the desk and jumped to his feet. "And she dragged you all the way from Pemberley for this reason? Tell me you didn't know before you set-out. Please."

"I knew enough to guess the rest," Darcy admitted.

"And you left Elizabeth, knowing that I am fully able to make my own decisions? That I am a man of the world who has led men into battle under my assessment of the risks we were to face and the chances of success?" Fitzwilliam asked incredulously.

"Your head has obviously been turned by a charming woman. You do not want the locality making assumptions that will force you into an imprudent marriage."

"The locality? I take it from that you mean that buffoon, Collins?"

"Mrs. Collins has mentioned in a letter to Elizabeth that you seem to be getting along famously with Miss Bamber."

"Oh, well, in that case there must be a marriage instantly!" Fitzwilliam said sarcastically. "We cannot have the sanctimonious fool spreading rumours, can we?"

"It wouldn't do Miss Bamber's reputation any good."

"Let me worry about Prudence's good name. You go back and take care of your wife."

"Prudence? You are on terms of using given names?"

"We use Anne's given names, so why not Prudence's?" Fitzwilliam demanded.

"We have known Anne our whole lives."

"We would have known Prudence a lot longer if not for Aunt Catherine's selfishness. Her father wrote when her mother died, asking for the grieving girl to have a visit, but Aunt Catherine refused. She only wants her near now because of the lack of companion for Anne."

"Aunt Catherine has admitted that she is looking for a position for the girl."

"And yet she's been told by Prudence that she is not looking to be situated as a companion."

"It's the best she could hope for in the circumstances," Darcy pointed out. "She cannot expect to make a good match with her background. You must see that Fitzwilliam."

"I see nothing of the sort," Fitzwilliam snarled at his cousin. It was the first time Darcy had seen real anger in his cousin's face, and it made him pause.

"You cannot make a match of it, Fitzwilliam. You need to marry a woman with funds. You know that," Darcy said gently.

"Don't you think I'm fully aware of that? It is the thing that keeps me lying awake at night!"

"I sympathise with your feelings. I truly do, but you cannot afford to marry her."

"I can if I'm prepared to get off my high horse and retrench," Fitzwilliam retorted.

"You would be happy for the first year, but what happens when the children start to arrive? What then, Cousin? Would your infatuation, love even, survive struggling to feed the many mouths you'll create together?"

"That is our decision to make. It's of no one else's concern."

"Have you spoken to her about it?"

"No."

"Does she know of your feelings?"

"Possibly not to their full extent," Fitzwilliam admitted.

"Then I beseech you to think carefully. You come from the top of society. Don't let us witness your fall because of a beguiling woman."

"It is more than that."

"At least think more about it."

"As I think of little else, that is an easy promise to make."

"In that case, I can ask no more," Darcy said. "I just hope you will come to realise what those of us who care for you have realised. You'll be happier in the long run."

"Are you sure about that?"

"Of course. I am not here because of malice or the wish to cause you angst. I do have your best interests at heart."

"I seem to recall your dislike at Aunt Catherine's interference in your life, yet it seems you consider it is acceptable in my case," Fitzwilliam said, reminding his cousin of the time Lady Catherine took it upon herself to visit Elizabeth at her home. It was with the intention of warning off Elizabeth from accepting any proposal. Instead of the outcome Lady Catherine desired, it actually gave Darcy hope and was the catalyst for Darcy returning to Elizabeth's neighbourhood.

"True. But I hadn't the same considerations as you have. I have persuaded Aunt Catherine not to write to your parents to advise them of your situation."

"Good God! Can the woman not leave anyone alone? Must she always interfere?"

"She has little else to do," Darcy admitted.

Fitzwilliam walked to the door of the study. He needed to get away from his cousin, the first time he had ever felt like that with Darcy.

"I'd just like to make one thing clear," he said, his hand on the door handle.

"What?"

"It is not an infatuation. I am actually deeply in love with her, and I have never felt like this about anyone else I have ever met. I doubt I shall ever feel this way again."

"Then I am truly sorry," Darcy admitted before his cousin left him alone.

Chapter 10

Prudence knew the reason Darcy had been brought in was something to do with herself. Fitzwilliam hadn't sought her out all day, even though he knew she wished to speak to him. Now at the evening meal they were seated at opposite ends of the table, and by the looks of him, he was deeply upset.

It put her in no mood to be congenial towards Darcy. A pity he was seated next to her.

Darcy could feel the animosity radiating from Prudence and aimed in his direction. He couldn't blame her in some respects, but he still congratulated himself on achieving his aim with Fitzwilliam. He could envisage the lifestyle Fitzwilliam would be forced to endure if he made an imprudent marriage that a man blinded with love could not see.

He decided to try to mend the shaky start they'd shared. "Your features remind me of my mother. Your resemblance to her is quite marked."

"Yes. Fitzwilliam has mentioned it," Prudence said, remembering with fondness that morning in the study.

"My own sister looks less like my mother than you do. Strange how we resemble different members of the family. It seems we are all to take after our father's side, apart from yourself."

"Ironic, is it not?" Prudence asked.

"A little. Does your father have family in Manchester?"

"Yes. He was born there and has three brothers," Prudence said coolly.

"Are they all in the industry?"

"Of course. Most people in Manchester have some connection to the cotton industry. It isn't the cotton capital of the world in name alone."

"Quite. He must have seen many changes."

"There has been a lot of growth. Not all of it good," Prudence admitted.

"Our aunt says you don't live in the centre of town."

"No. It's not too wearisome of a journey, but we have the benefit of being surrounded by greenery. Aunt Catherine says that your estate is the finest in Derbyshire."

"I am sure the Duke of Devonshire would have something to say on that score," Darcy said with a smile. "His estate at Chatsworth is far grander than Pemberley, but I prefer the location of my home."

"Yes. I can understand that. It's been a pleasure to visit Rosings, but I would not like to live here. It is too quiet for my tastes. I'm not used to being idle."

"Tell me. How do you fill your days?"

Lady Catherine stood to indicate her withdrawal, and Prudence looked at Darcy with a thin smile. "You shall have to wait until another day before I have the opportunity to shock you as to my daily routine," she said. "Please excuse me."

Darcy waited until he was left alone with his cousin. "I hear Mr. and Mrs. Collins are to join us."

"The evening has got even brighter," Fitzwilliam responded.

"Too harsh, Fitzwilliam. Come. You will rally," Darcy coaxed.

Fitzwilliam stood. "Do you know something, Cousin. I don't think I shall. Please send my apologies to Aunt Catherine. I have the urge to find a quiet corner and empty the contents of a decanter of brandy."

Darcy watched as his cousin left the room. It was worse than he thought. Fitzwilliam was acting in some respects as he had done when Elizabeth had turned down his first proposal. He'd not known what to do with himself. Sighing, he stood. He would have to join the ladies without the expectation of Fitzwilliam's easy banter and laughter. That he had partly caused his cousin's withdrawal made him feel remorse at being the one to give pain to another. Yes, it had been Aunt Catherine who had issued the express, but he hadn't needed to respond to it. For one who had suffered as a result of an uneasy route to happiness, he could only be saddened at his involvement in inflicting upset on one who meant so much to him.

That he thought it was right to point out the error of Fitzwilliam's judgement did not completely assuage the guilt.

Fitzwilliam would come to see they had been right.

*

Prudence was raging. She hardly ever lost her temper, but it was bubbling under the surface now as she marched across the small area of her bedchamber.

Only her inbred constraints prevented her from banging on Fitzwilliam's door and demanding he be honest with her.

98

She sighed. She didn't need him to say anything. They'd been irresponsible in betraying their affection for each other, and Aunt Catherine had reacted to it. Prudence was not a fool; she didn't need an explanation of the situation to work out what had gone on. Darcy had been brought in to warn Fitzwilliam away from her.

He might be willing to allow family members to interfere with his life, but she had no such considerations when making life choices.

All of a sudden, the familiarity of her home and friends seemed too far away, and she longed for a return to all that was precious to her. Only there could she start to feel something other than let down and disappointed at the way Fitzwilliam, the man she loved, had capitulated.

The following morning saw Prudence looking tired from a restless night. An air of discomfort and unhappiness settled on the group as a whole.

She'd taken Anne out, and although the quiet cousin had done all she could to rally Prudence, there had been no changing the sombre mood. Gathering together in the drawing room, it was left to Lady Catherine to lead the conversation.

Turning to Prudence, she smiled at her niece. "I have received some news in this morning's post that I know you will appreciate."

"Has Papa written to you?" Prudence asked hopefully.

"No. Better than that, although I'm sure you will wish to write to him with your news," Lady Catherine said.

"Oh?"

"An old friend, Mrs. Beattie has been looking for a companion for her mother. The lady is of a peculiar nature, so needs someone with a strong character who can be caregiver and offer guidance when necessary. I have been in communication with Mrs. Beattie, and she agrees that you sound like the perfect person for the role," Lady Catherine said very pleased with herself.

"Me? I thank you, but as I have mentioned in previous conversations, I am not looking for a role of any kind," Prudence said, her tone stiff.

"Nonsense, child," Lady Catherine waved her hand in dismissal. "It is the perfect position with a good family."

"Can I ask, apart from giving me the chamber of the previous companion you employed, what has given you the impression that I seek such a role?" Prudence asked.

"You've been placed in a servant's chamber?" Fitzwilliam asked in astonishment.

"It was the most suitable room for her," Lady Catherine said to her nephew, but even Darcy had looked astounded at Prudence's words.

"As the poor relation," Prudence offered, fire in her eyes, her mouth in a grim line.

"I have taken you in out of the goodness of my heart."

"To replace a servant. You've managed to presume I am a poor relation yet not paid me when I have stepped into a servant's role," Prudence pointed out, but then she turned to Anne. "But do not think I begrudge a moment spent in your company, Cousin. I have loved spending time with you. You are a darling and already very dear to me."

"As you are to me," Anne confessed.

"Thank you."

"This is stupidity. You have been welcomed into my home as my nephews have been."

"Have you ever interfered in their lives without them seeking your help?"

"Yes," Fitzwilliam responded, unable to stop the glare aimed in his aunt's direction. "Well, you did with Darcy."

Prudence turned to him. "Our cousin apparently stood up for his own wishes in that instance, did he not? And yet you haven't expressed your wishes to our aunt, have you Fitzwilliam? You faced the French numerous times, but when it came down to it, you did not fight for what you wanted, did you? Or was it a dalliance to entertain you while you rusticated?"

"An alliance with you? Of course he wasn't serious about a liaison with you, child! Be serious! As if there could be a match between you," Lady Catherine interjected before Fitzwilliam had time to respond.

Prudence stood. "Thank you for your hospitality. I shall be leaving within the hour. Please allow me to take your carriage to Westerham and from there I shall make my own way home."

"Prudence, no!" Fitzwilliam said headedly. "You cannot travel to Manchester alone."

"Why not? I have managed without a maid whilst I have been here, apart from when Anne was kind enough to share her own maid. I have not had the courtesy of being offered an escort on any of my outings whilst in residence, so why should this be different? After all, I come from the cotton mills, remember? We are made of sturdy stuff and can only aspire to become a companion, and that is if I am lucky," Prudence said with derision.

"Ungrateful, insolent girl! Don't think I shall be opening my home to you again!" Lady Catherine exclaimed.

"I would never accept an invitation from a woman so meddlesome and presumptuous as yourself, madam," Prudence said.

"I think you've said enough," Darcy cautioned.

Prudence turned to Darcy, her eyes flashing. "You are probably right, Cousin, but I am going to continue nonetheless," Prudence snapped. "How dare you come here and interfere with something that had nothing to do with you and you knew very little about! What gave you the right to interfere with something that was none of your concern? And you must have known that you could not possibly have had all of the details?"

"I knew all I needed to know," Darcy responded at his most quelling.

"Oh, you did, did you?" Prudence mocked. She gripped the back of a chair for support for she was shaking with anger. "Yesterday I was going to speak to Fitzwilliam and tell him the truth of my background. You see, my father, in his innocence, did not want me to appear gauche or at a disadvantage when I first arrived, so he was not honest about my situation. He is astute enough to be aware that the aristocracy does not like to hear about success from those of us in trade."

"Your father is a cotton worker," Lady Catherine said.

"Technically, I suppose you could say so. The reality of the situation is that my father is a mill owner. Of two mills actually," Prudence said with pride. "You made the presumption he was a cotton worker. The same way you presumed I'd be grateful if you obtained a position for me."

Darcy's eyes flew to his aunt's, but she was looking aghast at Prudence. Darcy's mouth set in a grim line. He should have known better. He had been played for a fool, used as a puppet by his aunt.

"What do you mean by this?" Lady Catherine demanded.

"That you presumed a lot about my father and I, and because of your preconceived ideas, you forgot to find out the reality of our situation. The truth of the matter, Aunt, is that I am an heiress to a substantial amount. My father was not always as wealthy as he is today, but even when he married my mother, he was able to give her a good living. Our house is not as grand as Rosings. After all we have only ten bedchambers to boast of, but it is within its own grounds. We have a handsome stable and are thought to be one of the richest families in the area."

"I knew you were richer than Mama thought!" Anne said with glee. "The quality of your clothes was far too fine, but nobody seemed to really take note except me."

"I did," Fitzwilliam said quietly.

"But you didn't really see, did you?" Prudence asked him sadly. "The evidence was there but you did not believe it. I mentioned I had been taught by a governess, for goodness sake! What more of a clue did you need? I suppose as far as you were concerned, I was the poor relative, and that was that."

"I'm sorry," Fitzwilliam said.

"So am I. More than I ever thought possible. I wanted to be liked because of who I was, not because of the money I have. I now realise it was never going to be so. It is time for me to leave." Prudence walked to the door, but was stayed by her aunt's words.

"How much are you worth?"

She smiled bitterly. "It truly is all about the money, isn't it?" she asked sadly. "Not that it matters, but I shall bring eight thousand a year to any marriage I agree to."

"But that is more than Anne has!" Lady Catherine exclaimed.

"Yes. Oh, and Aunt, just for your information. My jewels aren't paste. Only the finest creations are made for the daughter of Mr. Bamber. Nor are they the only ones I own. I have my own diamonds, rubies, and pearls, but I did not wish to carry them. I shall bid you all a good-bye, for I doubt that our paths will ever cross again."

Chapter 11

The room stilled when Prudence left. Lady Catherine looked as if to speak on numerous occasions, but the words didn't actually form on her lips.

Fitzwilliam eventually stood and looked at his aunt and cousin. "I hope you are both proud of yourselves. I cannot believe we have treated anyone like we have treated her, and she is related to us!"

"Fitzwilliam, we weren't to know," Darcy said quietly.

"It is just as she said, isn't it? You did not try to find out. The laughable result in all of this is that it doesn't matter to you two. You," he pointed at Lady Catherine, "will continue to lord it over your locality, and fools that they are, they will bow down to you time and again, and you," he pointed at Darcy. "Will return to your lovely wife and family in your big house without a care in the world. In the meantime, you have managed to insult in every way possible a woman who is worth ten of either of you. Oh, and you have made sure that I will never marry the woman that I'm deeply in love with. A fine day's work. I hope you're both proud of your meddling. I too shall be leaving shortly, and although I might be forced to meet with you in the future, it shan't be for a very long time."

Darcy stood. "Fitzwilliam, do not leave like this."

"How can it be remedied, Darcy? How can we persuade Prudence, after her receiving such ill-treatment here, that any one of us is genuine? For I wouldn't believe us, if I were she," Fitzwilliam said. "You have ruined the one chance I had of real happiness. Do you know that for once I did not care that we were to be poor? All I wanted was to spend the rest of my life with a woman who can make me laugh, make me want to kiss her, and to whom I confessed things I've never spoken to another living being."

"Tell me what to do to make it right."

"There is nothing any of us can do, is there? If we try and make amends, she would reject our appeal. If by some miracle we could convince her of our sorrow and beg her forgiveness, she would never really believe that it wasn't purely because she had told us about the money. As she said, it all comes down to that."

"Surely it is worth a try, Cousin?" Anne asked.

"I have told her often enough that I need to marry for money, and I could, no, I should have already proposed, but I did not. How the devil can I convince her that my regard is genuine?"

Darcy had never seen his cousin look so wretched. "She will believe you in time."

"I would not insult her by trying to convince her of any falsehoods I might utter. I've told her enough times that I needed a fortune, and I panicked when we kissed in the long gallery and she mentioned that we could be forced to marry. That does not sound like a man to be easily forgiven."

"You have kissed?"

"Yes. A number of times. You see, Darcy, I was not lying when I said I loved her."

"In that case, I am truly sorry," Darcy said.

"It is a little late for that," Fitzwilliam said walking out of the room.

*

Prudence was glad to secure a place on the stage. Being surrounded by people meant she had to force herself to suppress the emotions that threatened to overwhelm her.

She had been so angry with them all, it had helped to carry her through the packing of her portmanteau. Even when Anne had sought her out, she'd managed to maintain her control.

Anne had been in tears as she'd watched Prudence gathering her clothing. "Please do not leave. We can sort this out. I know Darcy is sorry, and Fitzwilliam is wretched."

"It is too late, Anne. Too much has been said that cannot be unsaid," Prudence responded, not looking at her cousin.

"But I will miss you!"

Prudence paused and wrapped Anne in an embrace. "And I will miss you. I would invite you to visit me, but I know you would never be allowed."

"Will you write? Please?"

"Yes. Of course. But do not be surprised if my letters do not reach you. I feel your mother will not encourage any contact between us."

"I shall inform the staff that my letters shall be kept separate from now on!" Anne said. "It is about time Mother realises she cannot interfere without consequences."

"Anne, don't make your life difficult on my account," Prudence said gently.

"I will never forgive mother for how she has treated you. But it is more than that. She will ruin my life if I let her. I have never been so happy as I have since your arrival at Rosings. You have shown me how to enjoy myself, and I do not wish for that to stop," Anne said.

Prudence was impressed with the determined set of her cousin's chin and smiled at the words. "I wish you all the courage in the world. I hope you learn how to maintain what you have achieved recently. Remember this Anne. I might have made the suggestions, but it was you who took the risk in agreeing to the schemes. If you had been caught, your mother's wrath would have been aimed in both our directions, which I think you realised."

"Yes. I knew she would seek to make me regret my decisions. Usually she achieves it through making me feel guilty and unsure of myself," Anne admitted.

Enveloping Anne in a second embrace, Prudence squeezed her. "Please believe me when I say you are a wonderful person, and underneath your fragile appearance, you are a very strong young woman."

"I am not self-assured. Nor impregnable, as I would wish to be."

"Of course, you are!" Prudence insisted, holding her cousin at arm's length. "I buckled after being with your mother for only a few weeks. You have stood her barrages for years!"

Anne laughed and moved away from Prudence, wiping her wet eyes on her handkerchief. "I suppose so, if you put it like that. Oh, Prudence! I shall miss you so very much!"

"Do not say anymore, Anne, for I am close to turning into a watering pot, and I refuse to be a wet goose."

"Can you not forgive Fitzwilliam? We both know his feelings are sincere."

Slamming down the lid of the portmanteau, Prudence stood, picking up her pelisse and throwing it roughly around her shoulders before slipping her arms into the sleeves. "No. It's more than that. Marriages go through troubles, and I need to have a husband by my side who will support me and defend me when necessary. Fitzwilliam did not stand up to them when it mattered, and that I cannot forgive."

"Then I am sorry for the both of you, for I have never seen him so happy as when he is in your company."

"He's the type to be jovial wherever he goes."

"Yes. He has a pleasant nature," Anne admitted. "But he has never glowed before. He is truly besotted with you."

"It's time for me to go," Prudence said, not reacting to Anne's words. "Please let me leave without your waving me off. I wish to remain brave."

Anne sniffed, but capitulated to Prudence's wishes. A footman entered the room and carried the luggage downstairs. They exchanged a brief final embrace, and Prudence quickly left the room without looking back.

Walking downstairs, she was relieved to see it empty but stiffened when the door to the study opened.

Darcy walked out of the room. "Miss Bamber. Cousin, would you be good enough to give me a moment before you leave? Please?"

Prudence sighed. "I cannot see that there is anything left to say to each other."

"I would like to apologise," Darcy said. "I should have listened to my wife more and my aunt less."

"I think I should like your wife," Prudence said. There was a slight twitch of her lips, but she was in no mood to smile.

"She is wiser than I. I should have learned that by now, but it seems I am still to be a dunderhead," Darcy admitted. "I am genuinely apologetic that I jumped to the same conclusions that my aunt did. I have no excuse to make."

"In the long-term, it does not affect me," Prudence lied. She inwardly doubted if she would ever be the same. "But I think you owe a bigger apology to Fitzwilliam. You did not know me, so presuming much is not a surprise, but you have known him all your life. Your behaviour and interference towards him is less forgivable, but no doubt the relationship you have shared will help to ease the pain you have caused. We do not have that connection, nor history."

"And that is a regret. I had hoped to know you better." Darcy walked across to Prudence. "I shall beg Fitzwilliam's forgiveness again and again, but I also beg yours. I know when I am in the wrong, and I wish you would tell me how to make amends. Could I persuade you to visit Pemberley and meet my wife? We could try again?"

"Perhaps. I am not in the right frame of mind to think sensibly at the moment," Prudence admitted. "When I have returned to normality, I am sure I shall rally."

"I hope so. I would like you to visit."

"There's one thing you can do as a service, if you are willing."

"Anything."

"Do not abandon Anne. She has been speaking her mind to her mother, something I am led to believe is a recent occurrence. I would hate to think she returns to being completely browbeaten by our aunt. I think Anne would be less inclined to ill health if she had more freedom. Perhaps you could invite her to Pemberley?" Prudence asked.

"Aunt Catherine would never countenance it," Darcy laughed.

"And you are guided by her every command?"

"When it is to do with her only daughter, it is more difficult to overcome her wishes."

"Then Anne is doomed to be miserable. A real pity, for she is a lovely girl. Goodbye, Mr. Darcy. It has been an interesting experience," Prudence said with a slight curtsy before walking to the open door.

She let the tears fall when the carriage left Rosings behind. It was inevitable that once free of the tension, she would allow herself some time to wallow in feelings of despair. He had not tried to stop her. She was sure it would not have changed her mind, but it stung that he'd allowed her to leave without trying to see her. She was contradictory, and she cursed herself for it, but she could not alter her wish to have seen him one last time.

Now she was on the stage, surrounded by people, and longing to reach home.

*

Days of travel and the strain of being alert to everything going on around her and the constant worry of falling prey to anyone willing to take advantage of a lone female had resulted in Prudence arriving home with a severe headache and a churning stomach.

On the way to her aunt, a maid had travelled with her in her father's carriage until Lady Catherine's carriage had collected her from Westerham. Prudence now realised that it was because her aunt had presumed she would be travelling on the stage. On leaving, she had not wished to wait until her father's carriage could be sent, as there had been weeks left of the planned visit, hence she'd taken the stage.

Tipping the coachmen well had ensured they had looked out for the quiet young lady who was travelling such a distance with them. When she was handed to a different coach, a quiet word in the driver's ear by the one she was leaving ensured that her unobtrusive protection continued. It helped a little.

Arriving in Manchester, she breathed a sigh of relief. She was once more in familiar territory. Hiring a hack, she sent her portmanteau to be delivered home.

Her father would be working in one of his mills, and she wanted the busy environment to take off some of the focus her early arrival would cause. She set-off walking in the direction of Bamber mills.

Chapter 12

Mr. Bamber looked up from his large desk at the familiar knock on the window of the office door.

"Prudence? What the devil are you doing here? What's wrong?" Mr. Bamber asked, immediately rising from his seat to greet his daughter.

"Hello, Papa," Prudence smiled. "I found I missed you too much. It is too quiet for me in the country."

"Nonsense! What's the real reason you have returned? Not that I am displeased to see you. It fair warms my heart to have you back home. The place has been like a graveyard without you buzzing about the house," Mr. Bamber said.

"I am glad to hear I was missed," Prudence said, kissing her father's cheek. "More than once I longed to have your counsel, I can tell you."

"Not up to snuff, were they?" Mr. Bamber asked gently.

"A couple of them were," Prudence admitted. "But the others made some spectacular assumptions."

"Ah, I feared as much, but I hoped it would not be so. Your mama was the best out of the bunch of them. Never mind. You are home now, and that is something I am thankful for," Mr. Bamber said.

"I am equally so," Prudence said. "Now how can I be of use?"

"You should go home and rest."

"I'm no fine lady who needs to be pampered. I'm much happier when I'm useful."

"You will do for me, lass. You will do for me!"

*

When the evening gloom had settled across the chimneys and roof tops of Manchester, Prudence travelled with her father back to their home. It was on the outskirts of the city, a place called Stretford. An agricultural and hand-weaving region, which many of the mill owners had moved into because of its position between the River Mersey and the River Irwell. The plain seemed to protect its residents from the smoke and smog created by Manchester city centre, making it even more attractive to those able to escape the unhealthy environment.

Prudence smiled as she stepped out of the carriage when it came to a stop outside the large stone doorway. The butler was there to welcome them home.

"Miss Bamber, it is a pleasure to see you home," the butler, Walsh, said.

"It is good to be here," Prudence answered. She glanced upwards at the house that had been her home as far back as she could remember. It was not as grand as Rosings, but it was a large house, and every brick was precious to her.

Walking into her chamber, she was reminded that she hadn't bathed in days and was extremely travel weary. Her maid, Bessie, was there to greet her; everything had been put away, and a bath was being drawn. Theirs was one of the more modern houses with a separate room for bathing and ablutions.

"Oh, it is a relief to be home, Bessie," Prudence said as she was helped to undress. "The houses of my family might be grand but my goodness they are cold places! And as for using the pot under the bed, or the tin bath, I can tell you, they can keep their fancy houses! Give me a newly built one any day!"

Prudence soaked in the warm bath, the fire roaring in the grate and let her herself relax for the first time in days. She would struggle to forget a pair of laughing green eyes, but sighing, she resigned herself to the fact that she had little choice.

After bathing and dressing, she entered the drawing room before sitting down to supper. Mr. Bamber greeted his daughter by handing her a glass of wine. "Was it really bad?"

Smiling Prudence took a sip of the rich, red liquid. "Perhaps we should have been honest about our situation. I have to take some responsibility that they were able to jump to their own conclusions because we were not truthful from the start."

"I wanted them to see you as the lovely person you are, not as an amount of money. I wished for your viscount to fall in love with you before he found out you were an heiress."

Prudence laughed. "There were no viscounts, Papa, and they would not have been interested in me if there had been. I get the distinct impression that they want their wives to be meek and mild. Except for the likes of Aunt Catherine. I am not sure she has ever been timid. She certainly tried to rule her household in exactly the way she considered best."

"Sounds like a dragon. Thank goodness I did not marry her!"

"I don't think there would have ever been any danger of that," Prudence smiled.

"I wanted you to know your other family, as your mother would have wished. It was my greatest sadness that she died without reconciling with them. It was hard for her to be away from her social circle, but I shall be forever grateful that she was prepared to leave them for me," Mr. Bamber said, his eyes a little misty.

"How did you know she was the one for you?" Prudence asked. She loved to hear about her parents' romance, but she had other motives now.

"It is strange to say, but I think from almost the first time I met her, I knew there would be no other for me," Mr. Bamber admitted. "She said she felt the pull just as much as I did."

"Did you ever doubt your choice? You must have had a difficult time of it at the start."

"It wasn't easy, but we had each other, and that was all that was important. We could face the difficulties and censure because we were together."

Prudence sighed. Her father was right, of course. A pair would always be stronger together. It is what should have happened between Colonel Fitzwilliam and herself, if there had been true feeling and understanding. Unfortunately for her bruised heart, any deep affection had been one-sided, and she was the one still suffering.

"Let's have a party," Mr. Bamber said, changing the subject.

"Why?"

"Because you have returned home. Why should I need an excuse? Plan a dinner and arrange some dancing."

"As you wish, Papa," Prudence said.

*

The evening of the party arrived three weeks after Prudence's unexpected return home. She still awoke with a feeling of disquiet, and no matter what she did, she could not shake it off.

The house was fully prepared to receive its twenty guests for the evening. Mill owners very often socialised. Their working hours might be long, but they did not neglect opportunities for enjoying themselves either.

The long dining table had been set with additional leaves to extend it to its full length. The pristine white tablecloth could hardly be seen because of the range of cutlery, dishes, and glassware, glistening in the candlelight. The centre would be filled with every kind of delight from soups to venison, beef, mullet with cardinal sauce, turkey, lamb cutlets, marrow pate, and meringues a la crème, to name just a few of the twenty-five dishes to be served. Mr. Bamber enjoyed entertaining and always ensured his guests left his table feeling the need to dance some of the excesses away.

Prudence dressed with care, choosing a lemon-colored dress with the most delicate lace edging. The dress was embroidered with rich yellow and white flowers along the hem and the edges of the small puff sleeves. She wore pearls, feeling the delicate necklace was appropriate for the evening.

Busy with greeting guests and circulating in the drawing room where everyone gathered before being taken into the dining room, she could not help but wish that Fitzwilliam could be there. How he had become so important in such a short amount of time, she had wondered when still at Rosings. Now she wondered how she could possibly still be repining over his loss.

Withdrawing with the ladies after everyone had enjoyed a sumptuous meal, Prudence was approached by another daughter of a mill owner, a Miss Selina Beauchamp.

"Miss Bamber, we missed you at last month's assembly," Selina said with a smile.

"I'm sure you were very well entertained," Prudence said politely. She had never really liked Selina, always sensing an unfriendly undercurrent from the young woman. "But I shall be at the next."

"Glad to hear it. We thought you might have had your head turned by one of your fine relatives and decided to stay with them."

"We are both Manchester girls. I would as likely leave as you would."

"I would leave without a glance backwards," Selina said with a slight note of derision as she looked around the room with an expression of disdain. "I certainly do not see my future amongst the grime of Manchester."

"That is the same place that has given us our fortunes and lifestyle," Prudence pointed out.

"The same way the aristocracy made their money in the sugar plantations, but you do not see many of them living there."

Prudence had to acknowledge her comment. "Are you hoping to marry someone from outside our circle?"

"Aren't we all?"

"To be fair, I had not given it any serious consideration," Prudence said. She fiddled with her skirt, not wishing to reveal any of her feelings on what, or who, had changed her mind about the married state.

"I shan't be staying in this area. The first opportunity I get, I shall be gone."

"I was recently told that, by our age, the aristocracy would consider us on the shelf, confirmed spinsters," Prudence pointed out.

"One can buy anything with money. Especially a husband. I am to travel in the Spring, and I will never return." Selina stood and started to walk away. "I'd advise you to do the same, Miss Bamber. You are a little older than I, and it is beginning to show."

Prudence could have laughed at Selina, but at that moment, a touch of her elbow notified her that the butler wished to speak to her discreetly.

"Miss Bamber, there is a gentleman wishing to speak to you. I suggested he call back in the morning, but he has asked could he sleep in the servant's quarters. I would normally send him away under no doubt of my opinion of his impertinence, but he says he is from Rosings Park."

"From Rosings?" Prudence asked, her colour rising. "And what is his name?"

"Mr. Huxley."

Chapter 13

Prudence immediately approached a Mrs. Warburton, one of the older ladies of her acquaintance and a trusted friend. "Would I ask too much if I asked you to organise the dancing once the gentlemen join the ladies? I have an unexpected visitor from my aunt's home, and I need to speak with him," she quietly explained.

"Of course, my dear. You do what you need to do, and I shall take control here. Will your father be joining you?"

"Not at this stage," Prudence said. "I shall send for him if I need to."

"I hope everything is well, but don't worry about us. We shall entertain ourselves."

"Thank you," Prudence said, before unobtrusively leaving the room. She followed her butler into the small morning room where Mr. Huxley stood by a sofa, looking uncomfortable. He gripped his hat tightly in his hands, and he looked travel weary and tired.

Prudence nodded dismissal to the butler, who closed the door behind him when he left the room. Only then did Prudence break the silence.

"Mr. Huxley! Are my aunt and cousin well?"

"They are Miss Bamber. Perfectly well when I left them. Well mostly," Mr. Huxley gabbled.

"Please. Be seated. You look fit to drop. Let me get you a glass of brandy, and you can tell me what is happening. You are clearly out of sorts." Prudence was business-like, approaching a side cabinet and opening it to reveal glasses and three decanters of dark liquid. Filling a glass, she approached Mr. Huxley and handed him the drink.

"Thank you, Miss Bamber. It's been a heck of a few days," the weary man said, taking a large gulp.

"Tell me everything," Prudence instructed, sitting opposite him.

"I have been dismissed from Rosings without a reference. Without anything apart from the clothes I stand up in actually."

"What? No! What happened?"

"I was foolish, Miss. I'll own my stupidity in the situation. I replaced you in taking Miss Anne out every morning through the parkland. We both enjoyed it, and one day — I — well, I was a little foolish. I let my feelings get the better of me," Mr. Huxley admitted with a flush.

"Oh, dear," Prudence said. Her hands had become a little sweaty as she anticipated what was to come.

"Yes. Exactly," Mr. Huxley said with a grimace. "It was reported to Lady Catherine that I had been seen kissing Miss Anne's hand."

"With Anne's permission?"

"She didn't expect it but said she was glad I had done it," he said with a wistful smile. "We didn't know that we had been seen. Not until we returned to the house."

"Lady Catherine was not happy, I presume?"

"No. She sent me off after screaming at me that I'd abused her trust and her daughter. I did not set-out to fall in love with Miss Anne, I assure you."

"None of us can dictate for whom our feelings develop," Prudence admitted.

"I tried to hide them, but recently, I had thought that perhaps Miss Anne wasn't quite as indifferent as she should have been. Me being a servant."

Prudence smiled. He was a genuinely nice man, and Anne could do a lot worse than him. She was convinced he would treasure her cousin as she should be treasured. "Did you explain this to Lady Catherine?"

"I didn't get the chance, Miss. She had me thrown off the property. All my worldly goods are still there. I came with only the clothes I stood up in and the few pennies I had on my person."

"Dear God! How could she be so cruel?" Prudence exclaimed.

"She was angry. I understand that. She wanted more than I could ever offer for Miss Anne."

"But she made you destitute. I'm glad you came here. What made you decide to do so?"

"Miss Anne was crying and pleading with Lady Catherine, but she would not listen to her. In the end Miss Anne ran to me as I was being escorted by the footmen and told me to come to you. I have no family you see. There was no one else I could seek out," Mr. Huxley finished.

"Poor Anne. Poor you," Prudence said. "You are here now and can stay for as long as you need to. We shall think about the issue with regards to your reference tomorrow. I am sorry that I have to return to my guests, but I shall inform my father of your arrival."

"I wouldn't wish to get you in trouble, Miss."

"Not at all. We are not the type of people to turn someone away in their hour of need. You are my guest, and father will welcome you. Truly."

Ringing the bell, Prudence waited until the butler entered. "Mr. Huxley will be staying with us. He is travel weary and hungry, I'd imagine. Please arrange for a meal to be served to him in here while one of the guest chambers is prepared for him."

"Yes, Miss Bamber."

"Mr. Huxley, I am sure you would wish your clothing to be freshened up after your journey. Walsh, please arrange for some clothing. Mr. Huxley's luggage has become separated from him, and until it arrives, he will need some alternatives."

"Of course." The butler left the room to carry out his duties.

"Thank you. He must think it a strange affair, my arrival at such an hour," Mr. Huxley said, a flush on his cheeks.

"The servants here will not judge you," Prudence assured him. "Please do not distress yourself. You are safe and welcome."

"You cannot realise how much I value those words." Mr. Huxley looked exhausted and emotional.

Prudence decided that she had been away long enough and stood up. Mr. Huxley also stood. "Wait here," she said. "There will be food arriving soon. Take your time and rest. I don't expect to see you until very late in the morning. I hope our party will not disturb you too much."

Mr. Huxley bowed, his expression was serious and yet grateful.

Prudence left the room as a footman entered with a large tray laden with food. She smiled and thanked the servant before returning to her guests.

*

A late breakfast was served in the dining room the following morning. Prudence and her father were already seated when Mr. Huxley entered the large room. Not a trace of the previous night's activity remained to be seen. The room had returned to being a quiet, relaxing space.

"Ah, this must be young Huxley," Mr. Bamber said, standing and holding out his hand in greeting. "Good to see you, my boy. I take it you slept well?"

"Yes, sir. Thank you, sir, and thank you for your hospitality," Mr. Huxley said quickly.

"We always like receiving visitors, don't we, my sweet?" he asked Prudence, not waiting for a reply. "Now sit yourself down and tuck in. You will need a good breakfast in you if you are to spend the day with me."

Mr. Huxley took a seat at the dining table, smaller now the temporary leaves had been removed. He looked uncomfortable being in the dining room with the family, but Prudence offered him food so that his plate was soon overflowing with eggs, bread, steak and ham.

"I am to spend the day with you, sir?" he asked.

"Yes. Prudence says you have been cast off without a reference?"

"Yes, sir." Mr. Huxley's cheeks burned. He might be above thirty years in age, but to be dismissed in such a way had reduced him to feeling like a naughty schoolboy.

"We can get over that easy enough. Prudence here has told me a little about the size of the house you worked for. It must have taken a lot of hard work."

"I was busy. Lady Catherine likes things to be just so."

"Aye. It would be called fussy around here, but each to their own," Mr. Bamber said. "We need to sort out what's to be done with you now. I am happy to give you a reference, but I want to know how you work, first of all. If you have no objections, you will be working with me in the mill for a little while."

"Really?" Mr. Huxley asked. His fork had clattered to his plate, and he looked mortified at his gauche behaviour.

"I will pay you. Don't you worry. But you will be worked hard, so prepare yourself," Mr. Bamber warned good-naturedly.

"You do not need to pay me, sir. You are very kind. My needs are very small, but I — er — it's a little embarrassing, but if I could ask for just enough to secure some board somewhere," Mr. Huxley stammered.

"Why on earth would you need to board elsewhere when there are bedchambers a-plenty here?" Mr. Bamber asked.

"I do not wish to impose."

"Nonsense. You are here as our guest. Don't let me hear anymore silliness."

"No sir. Thank you, sir."

"And I will pay you for a hard day's work. Do not think you won't earn every penny, for I am likely as much a termagant as that aunt of our Prudence's is."

"You will soon realise that my father speaks his mind, just as much as Lady Catherine does, but with a little less maliciousness," Prudence said with a shake of her head at her father.

Mr. Huxley smiled at the pair. "In fear of sounding like a bumbling fool, thank you once again. I am extremely obliged."

"Oh, you will work hard. Do not be lulled into a false sense of security. I didn't get to own two mills by being a man who likes to take things easy."

"Now do not go frightening him, Papa!" Prudence laughed. "I will write to Anne today and tell her you have arrived safe and sound and are here to stay."

"Thank you, Miss. I do not want Miss Anne worrying. She can become ill so suddenly."

"She is stronger than she looks. Now, I must send my letter before I go out on morning calls. It is strange. I feel as if my time at Rosings is a distant memory."

"It wasn't the same after you left, Miss," Mr. Huxley said. "You took all the cheerfulness away with you. Mr. Darcy left for his home the morning after you departed, and Colonel Fitzwilliam soon returned to London. Miss Anne was in the doldrums, which was part of the reason I asked her to continue the morning rides out. I thought it would lift her spirits."

"I am glad you did. She needs to continue to build her strength. I only hope with both of us gone, she finds a way to ride out."

"I'm not sure Lady Catherine will ever let her leave her side again, Miss."

"No. Nor I," Prudence admitted sadly.

*

When the three gathered for their evening meal, it was as if the Bambers had a different guest staying with them. Mr. Huxley no longer seemed afraid of saying the wrong things but was full of what he had seen during the day.

"I never thought the mills were so big!" he exclaimed to Prudence. "They are bigger than any other building I've ever seen."

"Do not let Lady Catherine hear that. She will immediately order an extension of Rosings." Prudence smiled.

"She probably would. I could not believe the noise. It hardly ever ceased."

"I miss it when I'm not there," Mr. Bamber admitted.

"That is why I can never get you to visit anywhere outside of Manchester," Prudence admonished.

"Why would I want to go anywhere else when all I need is here?" There was genuine puzzlement on Mr. Bamber's face, at which Prudence laughed.

"You are incorrigible, Papa. You love it here, and yet you tried to send me away."

"That's because parents want what is best for our children."

"I am quite happy being in Stretford, thank you," Prudence said tartly.

"It was not as rural where your aunt lives."

"And look how bored I was there. I came home early." She noticed the curious look Mr. Huxley aimed in her direction, but she ignored it, hoping her father had not noticed it.

Unfortunately for Prudence, Mr. Bamber had noticed exactly what had passed, and two days later in a lull at the mill, he brought up the subject with Mr. Huxley.

"Which one of the gentlemen at Rosings has turned my girl's head? And before you start to deny it, I saw the look you gave her at supper the other night," Mr. Bamber said to the cornered Mr. Huxley.

The younger man sat heavily in his seat. "I will not lie to you, sir, but I wish you would not ask me anything."

"Unfortunately for you, my daughter has kept her feelings to herself since her return but has walked around the place with a haunted look in her eyes. Oh, she thinks she has kept it from me, but I saw the moment she walked through this door when she returned that something was amiss."

"She decided to leave quite suddenly," Mr. Huxley said hesitantly.

"I know that. Now don't start being all niffy-naffy with me. Tell me what is going on, and I will think all the better of you for it," Mr. Bamber said.

"Miss Prudence might not, though," Mr. Huxley pointed out.

Mr. Bamber chuckled. "Sometimes the silly chit thinks she knows best, but when she is hurting, I know for sure she does not." He sat on the edge of the large desk, close to Mr. Huxley. "Now, come, who was it turned her head? And why isn't there a marriage being announced?"

Mr. Huxley sank a little in his seat. He was astute enough to know he was fighting a losing battle trying to avoid speaking about what had happened at Rosings. Sighing he looked at Mr. Bamber. "Miss Bamber became very friendly with one of her cousins, Colonel Fitzwilliam."

"A colonel, eh? That's good. Something obviously did not go well, or I would probably be welcoming a new son by now. Which one of them erred?"

"I do not know all the details. I only know that their other cousin, Mr. Darcy, came to visit suddenly, as a result of a letter from Lady Catherine, and there was an almighty argument. For the first time, there seems to be a rift between Mr. Darcy and Colonel Fitzwilliam. It is very strange, for they've been as close as brothers over the years."

"Hmmm. Interesting. So Lady Catherine decided to interfere, did she? Hurt my girl in the process. Well it was my own doing. I was foolish enough to wish her to meet her family. Seems I might have caused more mischief than benefit."

"Miss Anne thinks a lot of Miss Bamber."

"Aye, my Prudence has talked about her cousin. Seems she became mighty fond of her. A pity it all went wrong. I knew there was something amiss. What is so special about this Colonel that they would not wish my daughter to marry him?"

Mr. Huxley stood up hurriedly and walked to the window. "Sir, it is not my place to say."

"I'm not going to reveal what you tell me. I just need to know what I inadvertently caused."

"Colonel Fitzwilliam comes from a good family, but he is a second son."

"Ah. He needs to marry for money," Mr. Bamber said realising the truth from Mr. Huxley's few words. "There is no need to say any more lad. I can imagine the rest. The fools. He would have had more blunt than he could spend if he had stayed loyal to my Prudence. Bet he is sick to his stomach now he knows who she is. I am presuming she told them the truth before she left?"

"Yes. I believe so."

"Good girl. Well, he will live to regret it, but I'm glad my girl did not end up with a man just interested in her money."

"He seemed extremely upset. I think he had real affection for Miss Bamber," Mr. Huxley said of the raging Colonel. His words to Darcy had been heard all through the ground floor of Rosings.

"Not enough though, or he would be here wouldn't he? Thank you for telling me. I will not forget your honesty."

"I did not have much of a choice, really, did I?" Mr. Huxley asked with a smile on his lips.

"No. None at all."

Chapter 14

Prudence knocked on the door of her father's study before walking into the room. It was the place where she had spent a lot of time when growing up, her father never really being far away from business.

She smiled on entering the study, as both her father and Mr. Huxley were bent over some documents spread out on the desk.

"Gentlemen, it is Sunday. A day of rest, surely?" she asked.

Mr. Huxley looked up guiltily. "I'm sorry, Miss Bamber. I just keep asking questions. The whole business is fascinating. I shall leave you."

"There is no need for that, lad," Mr. Bamber said good-naturedly, but he started to wrap up the papers.

"I shall take a walk in the gardens and think about what we have discussed." Mr. Huxley left the room with a bow to Prudence.

"Have you found yourself a protégé?" she asked with a smile in her voice.

"He is a bright lad. I bet your aunt is ruing the day she let him go. He is very capable. I know he will want to move on at some point, but I admit, I will miss him when he's gone even though he has only been with us for a short time."

"I have noticed since his arrival how I have been neglected. I remember the times you used to come home and talk to me about the mills. Now it is all Mr. Huxley," Prudence teased.

Mr. Bamber walked around the desk and held his hands out to his daughter. When she placed hers in his, he squeezed them. "You know full well you would glaze over if I spoke to you about business as often as I do with young Huxley."

"Perhaps a little. But I insist that you have a break. I don't want you wearing yourself out just because you have a playmate."

"Cheeky wench," Mr. Bamber said. He linked Prudence's arm through his own. "What have you got planned to brighten my Sunday?"

"I thought we could go for a ride along the river? You have been neglecting your favourite horse as well as your daughter."

"In that case I think we ought to," Mr. Bamber said.

They had walked into the hallway and were heading for the stairs when the sound of an approaching carriage halted their progress.

"Who would come calling at this hour?" Mr. Bamber asked.

"I have no idea, but there seems to be some commotion," Prudence said. It seemed as if there were shouts coming from the carriage, and she hurried to the door along with her father and the butler.

Faltering on the step of the house, Prudence frowned. "It's Lady Catherine's carriage!"

"Is it?" Mr. Bamber asked, but did not stop to speak further as the coachman had jumped down and was shouting for them to hurry. "What is it? What's amiss?"

"Miss Anne is very ill, sir!" the coachman shouted without preamble, flinging open the door of the carriage. "She needs a doctor at once!"

Prudence ran to the open door of the carriage, arriving before her father had reached the vehicle. She looked inside before quickly climbing in.

"Anne? Anne! It's Prudence. What is amiss?"

Anne was laid across the seat. Her pallor was sickly looking, a sheen of sweat making the whiteness of her skin glisten. Her eyelids flickered at Prudence's voice, but she did not respond further.

"Dear God, Anne. What have you done?" Prudence asked quietly before turning to the three worried faces at the open door. "We need to get her to a chamber immediately. Lift her out, but be gentle. She is not of a strong constitution. She needs a doctor immediately."

Anne was carried out and taken into the house. A footman was despatched to get the local doctor while Prudence followed her cousin upstairs.

"Miss…" the worried voice of the coachman made her pause.

"I'll need to speak to you very soon, but I need to settle Miss De Bourgh first." Receiving a nod of understanding at her words, she continued up the stairs.

Prudence and Mrs. Williams, the housekeeper, carefully undressed Anne and sponged her down to try to cool her skin. They worked together in silence until the doctor arrived.

After examining Anne, he stood, a frown firmly in place. "I don't know her history, but she seems very fragile. She has a fever, and it seems to have taken a firm hold. I'll give her some laudanum, and I advise she is not left alone. Try to keep her cool. But without knowing her previous complaints, I cannot offer any real hope. From the look of things, she is severely ill."

Prudence sucked in a breath before speaking. "Thank you. We shall care for her as best we can."

"I shall return in the morning, but if she should worsen…"

"We will send for you immediately," Prudence said. She waited until the doctor had administered the liquid. It was painful to watch how unresponsive Anne was.

The housekeeper led the doctor out the door, and Prudence rang the bell. A footman knocked on the door, and Prudence opened it. "Where is the coachman?"

"In the kitchen, Miss. He was a little shaken but has calmed down now."

"Good. Please have him sent to the morning room. I shall see him there in a few moments."

Prudence had decided on the smallest room so as not to intimidate the coachman. She needed to know the whole situation and quickly.

"I shall return soon," Prudence said once the housekeeper had returned to the room. "I will stay with Anne tonight."

"I can look after her overnight, Miss Prudence," the old retainer said quietly. "You look after her during the day when I have my other duties to fulfil."

"You'll be exhausted doing both."

"The days will seem long for you. Don't wear yourself out. I think we're going to have to learn patience and forbearance."

Prudence looked at Anne. She was so tiny and frail in the huge expanse of the bed. It grieved her to see her lovely cousin so ill. Setting her shoulders, she stepped away from the bed. "I shall return as soon as I can."

Walking into the morning room, Prudence was immediately joined by her father.

"Keen to find out what has been going on," Mr. Bamber said.

The coachman looked terrified, but Prudence smiled at him in encouragement. "Please take a seat. We would be grateful if you would tell us everything that has happened."

The coachman sank into a seat. "It has been a nightmare, Miss," he said. "I didn't know what to do."

"Start from how Miss de Bourgh came to leave Rosings. It's such a long distance from Manchester, and there seems to be just the two of you."

The coachman looked as if he were about to burst into tears. Mr. Bamber stood and poured a drink from the side table. "Here, get this down you. We can't have the two of you collapsing on us, or we will never get to the bottom of it," he said, but his tone was gentle.

"When Mr. Huxley was dismissed, the house was in an uproar," the coachman started. "I've been with the family for fifteen years, and I ain't ever seen anything like it," he continued. "Lady Catherine was screaming and shouting. Lady Anne was crying and shouting — yes shouting at her mama."

"Really?"

"Yes. Then Lady Catherine had some sort of spasm and had to be carried to her chamber."

"Is she well?" Prudence asked.

"I think so. I don't really know, to be honest with you, Miss. Lady Anne demanded that the coach be brought around, and she climbed into it as soon as I arrived at the front of the house. She insisted that I take her to her cousin in London."

"Which cousin? Did she pack a case?" Prudence asked.

"I don't know which she was intending to visit, if any. I think now that her aim was always to come here. There wasn't time for her to bring anything. It all happened very fast."

"Did she bring her abigail with her?"

"No, Miss."

"Good God!"

"What happened at the coaching houses you stopped at?" Mr. Bamber asked.

"I took control, asking Lady Anne to remain in the carriage, and I brought things to her. I also employed a maid, but she was very poor, and I had to send her back. Miss Anne had to do without female assistance."

"When did she tell you to bring her north? And what did you do overnight? My mind is racing, wondering how you managed to overcome these obstacles!"

"Lady Catherine always keeps a supply of money in the carriage. Hidden in case we get robbed. It's never used because she is rarely out after nightfall," the coachman admitted. "It gave us money to get through the tolls and buy refreshments. It was quite a few pounds."

"Thank goodness for that."

"Yes. Staying at the inns was more tricky. I had to make up all sorts of stories before they would accept a young lady unaccompanied. I slept outside her door to make sure she was safe, but we couldn't always stay in the best inns. I think some of the sheets might have been damp because she started looking pale the further we travelled."

"Oh, dear. She is not used to such activity, either," Prudence said.

"No. I tried to persuade her to turn around and go home, but she was insistent that we continue. She threatened that she would cast me off and drive the carriage herself."

Prudence could not stop her laugh from escaping. "I told her she had claws! Oh, Anne, why have you risked yourself so?"

"For the last two days we haven't stopped, day or night."

"You have travelled through the night?" Mr. Bamber exclaimed.

"Yes. I had to. Lady Anne was very ill, and I had to get her here. Every time I opened the carriage door to check on her, I sent up a prayer that she was still alive."

"Oh, you poor thing! You must be fit to drop!" Prudence said.

"Will she get better, Miss? I know she's poorly."

"We don't know as yet, but be assured that she will have the best care. You need to rest. I will arrange for a room for you and some food. Go to bed and don't get up until you are fully recovered. You have gone above and beyond your duty over these last few days."

"I know Lady Catherine will turn me off for not bringing Lady Anne home, but she was so upset Miss. I've never seen her so. She has always been a good girl. I wanted to take her to her cousin in the hope they would help her. It was only later that I began to realise who she was travelling to."

"I presume you do not mean me?" Prudence asked.

"No, Miss. Is it true that Mr. Huxley is here? Lady Anne said she had told him to come here."

"Yes. He's here."

"Thank goodness for that. At least it wasn't a complete fool's errand, if you'll beg my pardon, Miss."

"Of course. Thank you for not deserting her," Prudence said, and then ringing the bell, she gave instructions of what was to happen with the weary coachman.

When Mr. Bamber was once more alone with his daughter, he shook his head at her. "It seems we are to inherit most of Lady Catherine's servants if this is to continue."

"Papa, she travelled all the way from Kent on her own!"

"As did you," Mr. Bamber pointed out.

"I'm not a slip of a chit who has barely been out of her own county and has been cosseted for every minute of her life. There is little difference between us in age, but believe me, we are worlds apart in experience. Anything could have happened."

"At this moment in time, what could have happened is irrelevant. Getting her well will be task enough."

"Yes. What the devil are we to tell Mr. Huxley?"

Chapter 15

Mr. Huxley was devastated. He cursed and raged for a full ten minutes before calming himself enough to be the sensible man he normally was.

"What can I do to help her?" he asked.

"She shall be given the best care possible," Prudence assured him for the tenth time in as many minutes. "There is one thing I need to discuss with you though, and it shall not be an easy decision to make."

"What? I'll do anything I can."

"We need to decide who to contact to let them know Anne is here with us and ill. As much as I would not wish to have Lady Catherine arrive at my door, I feel she has the right to know what is going on."

"She does not deserve the daughter she has been blessed with." The words were said with gritted teeth. Mr. Huxley was standing in front of the fireplace, his knuckles white with gripping the marble edge.

"That may be so, but Anne is her daughter, and Lady Catherine has a right to know. My only hesitation is about the news that she was taken ill. I do not wish to add to her distress, though I have little affection for the woman."

"No. Nor I," Mr. Huxley admitted. He sighed. "Perhaps it would be best to write to Mr. Darcy? He has had quite a bit of involvement with the family over the years I have been employed there. Lady Catherine seeks his counsel on many things. You could perhaps write to him."

"That is the direction my own thoughts were tended," Prudence admitted. "He is the closest family to us and might wish to visit in place of Lady Catherine. I shall send him an express."

"Might I see Miss Anne?"

"I do not think it would be a good idea at the moment."

"I would not put her at any risk."

"I know. Believe me when I say it would be best waiting until she is a little better."

"And if she doesn't recover?"

"If I see a deterioration then I will send for you to say your goodbyes," Prudence promised. Mr. Huxley choked at her words but managed to turn it into a cough. Prudence stood and walked to him, resting her arm on his shoulder. "We are going to do our very best to bring her back to us."

"Thank you."

Prudence left the room, understanding that Mr. Huxley needed time to gather himself. When she saw Anne, she wanted to wail with despair, but such reactions would do Anne no good at all.

Walking into the study, she immediately took a piece of parchment out of the drawer, and dipping the quill in the ink stand, started to write.

Dear Mr. Darcy,

I am sending this express to you as the nearest relative and the one to whom Lady Catherine very often turns when she seeks advice.

Recent events have resulted in Anne following Mr. Huxley to our abode. It is a long story, and now is not the

140

time to divulge the details, but your imagination will probably reach the correct conclusion to the situation. Needless to say, it was a journey undertaken after an altercation with Lady Catherine. It appears our aunt had some sort of seizure — to what extent and how well she is at present, I am afraid I have no knowledge.

Anne travelled across country alone except for one member of staff, and although her coachman tried to protect her and do the best for her in the circumstances, she has arrived in Stretford dangerously ill.

You can be assured that she is receiving every level of care, but I must be honest and inform you that the doctor is not confident of a recovery at this stage. It grieves me to write this, for she is very dear to me even after such a short acquaintance.

I need to inform Lady Catherine of the matter, but as I am not aware of her state of health I thought it wisest to contact you in the first instance. If yourself or Aunt Catherine wishes to visit Anne, you will be made welcome.

Your cousin,
Prudence Bamber.

There it was. She had done the right thing by Anne. Even if Aunt Catherine arrived on her doorstep, she would welcome her. She would do anything that might help Anne.

Standing and ringing the bell, she handed the express to the footman and returned to her cousin's bedchamber.

*

The following seven days had to be the longest of Prudence's life. The whole household seemed to feel the tension, which seeped into every room.

Each person hovered whenever the doctor visited, which was often, hoping to hear a snippet of good news for the young woman they did not know, but who was fighting for her life under their roof. Their shoulders would sag when the housekeeper would show the doctor out and gently shake her head in the negative at the onlookers.

Prudence joined her father each night to eat supper with him. Mr. Huxley was company for her father, but she needed the small semblance of normality eating a meal at the dining table brought.

Each evening, she was greeted with the same words from Mr. Huxley. "Any improvement?"

And each time she had to give the same response. "No. I am sorry."

It was the eighth evening, and when Prudence entered the drawing room, Mr. Bamber shook his head at his daughter.

"You are losing weight, Prudence, and you are as pale as I have ever seen you. I insist you have a break from the sick room, or you will be joining your cousin."

"I'm fine, Papa. Truly."

"No, you are not. I won't stand by whilst you waste away. That will do neither yourself nor Anne any good."

They were interrupted by the entrance of the butler. "Sorry to disturb you, sir, but there is a gentleman at the door requesting to see Miss Prudence. He says he's a cousin."

Prudence's eyes flew to Mr. Huxley. "It must be Mr. Darcy." Turning to the butler, she said, "I'll see him in the study. I expect he will not have eaten. Please set another place for him at the dining table."

"I should come with you," Mr. Huxley said. "She followed me. I have some responsibility in this."

"No. Anne chose to follow you, and she is well over the age of consent. It was her own doing. Remain here. I am not hanging you out for anyone to blame you in all of this."

"If there are any problems, send me word, and cousin or no, I will send him packing," Mr. Bamber instructed.

"I doubt there will be any need for that." Prudence smiled at her father as she left the room. She hoped there would not be. She had not exactly departed on good terms with Darcy. Oh well, it appeared being a member of her mother's family was going to be constantly trying.

Walking into the study, shoulders set, expecting to see her cousin Darcy, she faltered on the threshold. "Colonel Fitzwilliam," she said in a surprised greeting.

"Cousin."

"I did not expect to see you, but I presume you are here in Mr. Darcy's stead?" Prudence had forced herself to continue into the room when she actually wanted to retreat somewhere far away. She had thought of Fitzwilliam so many times. She had ached to see him again, but now he was here, she had no idea how to act. He looked formal, wary even, and she imagined she did not look too different.

"Yes. He sent me an urgent message to check on Aunt Catherine."

"How is she?"

"Being as demanding as always, but from her sick room. I feel she is remaining within her chamber to demand pity from those around her rather than out of necessity. She probably went into shock at Anne's outburst, but

143

underneath the tomfoolery she has embarked upon, she has a strong constitution," Fitzwilliam responded.

His eyes never left Prudence's, and the intensity of his stare was a little unnerving. "You have relayed your information to Mr. Darcy?"

"Yes. It was always my intention to travel here once I'd been to see how things were at Rosings. Mrs. Darcy is very close to her confinement now, and I did not wish Darcy to be away from home."

"That is very considerate of you. I knew of his situation, but I thought it best to send him the express."

"You could have contacted me," Fitzwilliam said quietly.

"No. I could not. It was hard enough contacting Darcy."

Fitzwilliam seemed to sag a little but continued to speak. "I knew when I arrived here there would be issues to sort out. Anne's health will dictate what happens next." He could feel the tension in the room just as much as Prudence could. He wanted to ask her how she had been: if it was through caring for Anne that she looked fagged, or if she was ailing herself. The thought that she might be ill had set his heart racing in panic. More than anything he wished to fall to his knees and beg forgiveness. Instead he stood ramrod straight and spoke in clipped terms.

"Anne is gravely ill," Prudence admitted.

Fitzwilliam paled. "Is it a hopeless case? Darcy said you had suggested it was."

"We honestly don't know, but there has been little change since she arrived here."

"May I see her?"

Prudence had refused Mr. Huxley admittance to Anne's room, but it was different for Fitzwilliam. He was almost like a brother to Anne, and she could not keep him away.

"Prepare yourself, Fitzwilliam. She has changed since you last saw her," Prudence said before turning on her heel and leading the way out of the room.

They walked in silence up the stairs and into the room in which Anne was lying motionless in the centre of the large four-poster bed. The housekeeper was tending to her, having taken over from Prudence for the night.

Fitzwilliam faltered when he saw his cousin. "She's always been small and fragile looking, but she looks…"

"I know," Prudence said gently. She had some sympathy for how he must be feeling. "Come. Speak to her."

"Speak to her?" Fitzwilliam asked in surprise.

"Yes. We do not know if she can hear anything, so we greet her and tell her about everything that is happening. Just in case she can."

Looking uncomfortable, Fitzwilliam approached the bed. "Hello, Anne," he said quietly. "It's Richard. I have come to see what all this fuss is about. You have been causing a bit of excitement, but everyone is absolutely fine at Rosings. There is nothing for you to worry about."

Prudence smiled at him for the gentle way he mentioned that Lady Catherine was well. She approved of his wording. "I am sure Anne will take comfort from hearing that, won't you Anne?"

As always there was no response, but Prudence had not expected one. Fitzwilliam looked at her for direction, and she indicated that they should leave the chamber.

"Good night, Anne," Fitzwilliam said. "I shall return on the morrow. I hope you are more in the mood for a chat then. I would so like to hear your voice again, Anne."

Leading the way once more, Prudence went down the stairs. "I shall arrange for a room to be prepared for you."

"Are you sure?" Fitzwilliam asked in surprise. "I expected to be staying at a local inn."

"Why would I not offer you hospitality?"

"Oh, something to do with the way we treated you during your visit with Aunt Catherine," came the dry response.

"As I said to Mr. Darcy, I would welcome Aunt Catherine if she came to visit Anne. Now is not the time for recriminations and going over what has happened. What's done is done," Prudence said. "My father and Mr. Huxley are in the drawing room."

"Mr. Huxley?"

"Yes. He's working for my father at the moment in order to obtain a reference as Aunt Catherine almost made him destitute."

"He behaved inappropriately towards Anne."

"Anne clearly did not think so."

Fitzwilliam reached out and touched Prudence's arm to stop her progress towards the drawing room. "Cousin — Prudence — you must see it was inappropriate of him? They are of a different social class."

"And yet it did not stop you when you thought you were kissing the daughter of a cotton worker, did it?" Prudence snapped. "I suggest your whole family look at your own conduct before starting to criticise someone else's."

Chapter 16

Prudence entered the drawing room and immediately Mr. Bamber and Mr. Huxley stood up. Mr. Huxley looked wary and unsure, but Prudence sent him a quick smile of reassurance.

"Papa, please allow me to introduce my cousin, Colonel Fitzwilliam." She was surprised at the assessing look her father shot in Fitzwilliam's direction, but she did not have the energy to ponder over it. "I've asked for another place to be set at the table, Cousin. I suggest we immediately remove ourselves to the dining room. Colonel Fitzwilliam's arrival has delayed supper a little, and you know how cook repines when her sauces are in danger of spoiling."

The gentlemen complied with Prudence's chivvying and entered the dining room. The butler looked relieved at their entrance; it seemed Prudence had been correct about the cook's angst.

Sitting down, Prudence resigned herself to an uncomfortable meal. Colonel Fitzwilliam and Mr. Huxley had barely exchanged a word, one looking daggers at the other, the other looking wary and unsure.

"You can speak to the doctor tomorrow, and he will tell you everything that has been done to ensure your cousin's comfort," Mr. Bamber said.

"I have already seen that she is being cared for extremely well," Colonel Fitzwilliam answered.

"Aye. Poor little mite. She's not been a robust girl, has she?"

"No. And I think my aunt did not encourage her to undertake anything that would have helped her constitution. It suited Aunt Catherine to keep Anne near her," Colonel Fitzwilliam admitted.

"A sad thing for the child," Mr. Bamber said with a shake of his head. "We all need to experience life as much as possible, especially when we are young."

"Quite so."

"I hear you have had an adventurous life yourself, sir."

"A little too adventurous at times," Colonel Fitzwilliam answered.

"Aye, I can only imagine. And what have you been doing since your return? Is life at home keeping you occupied?"

"There have been a few instances of unrest in your industry. We've been brought in to help keep the peace," Fitzwilliam answered.

"The workforce do not like the changes we mill owners bring in, but if we do not stay ahead of our business, someone else will beat us to it, and then we will all suffer," Mr. Bamber said.

"People are very often frightened of change or of things they do not understand," Prudence said. "They can make presumptions that are not always right."

Fitzwilliam looked down, supposing the comment was aimed at himself.

Prudence felt ashamed at the reaction her words caused. She cursed herself inwardly, she was better than making sly remarks. "How is Mrs. Darcy?"

"She is fine. I stopped at Pemberley on my way north," Fitzwilliam responded. "I think there shall be another Darcy very soon."

"I had hoped to meet her one day, but I don't think that will happen after the way things ended between myself and Mr. Darcy."

"Oh, I don't know," Fitzwilliam smiled. "Elizabeth is determined to see you as soon as she is able after her confinement. She is a very strong-minded woman. By far one of the best of my relatives."

"You might like to visit my mills in the coming days after you've sat with your cousin. A sick room is not the place for an active man like you," Mr. Bamber offered.

"That's very kind of you, sir. I would like that a great deal. I must admit I have never been this far north before and have never set foot in a mill."

"You will soon see we don't bite."

"You shall have to protect him from the mill girls, Papa. They will be on a par with the French army for their ability to cause fear in a young, single man."

"He will revel in it." Mr. Bamber laughed at the expression on Fitzwilliam's face.

*

Prudence was already seated with Anne when Fitzwilliam entered the sick room after he had breakfasted.

She looked up in surprise. "I did not expect to see you so soon."

"Your father was quite clear that he considered remaining in bed a wasteful time of the working day, so even though I am to remain here and not travel with himself into the mills, I was expected at breakfast," Fitzwilliam responded. He sat down with a sheepish look. "I admit, I haven't risen this early in many months."

"Well, I am sure Anne will be glad to know you are nearby."

Fitzwilliam reached over and took Anne's hand in his own. "Dear Anne, I wish you would come back to us. Life will not be the same without you in it. I, for one, would miss you so very much."

Prudence had to blink away the moisture the heartfelt words brought to her eyes. "I remain hopeful," she said quietly.

"It has been so long."

"Yes. But she isn't as robust as we are, so it will take her longer to fight off the fever. That is my hope anyway."

"I pray you are right. I promise to always supply you with whatever fancies you decide upon if you beat this fever, Anne."

"I hope for your sake that she cannot hear you, or you could be sorry you uttered those words."

Fitzwilliam smiled at Prudence, which made her insides flutter, much to her annoyance. "I would do my damndest to achieve my promise."

"I should think so."

"It is time I left you alone. I don't wish to tire Anne," Fitzwilliam said, standing up. "I shall visit again later." Walking to the door, he turned before opening it. "Miss Bamber?"

"Yes?"

"Our family are in your debt. All of us, and we thank you most sincerely."

"I am doing this for Anne."

"I understand and can expect no more, but I realise it must be costing you to be civil to the likes of Darcy and myself. I would probably struggle if our roles were reversed."

"Thankfully, they are not."

"Yes. Quite."

The door closed behind him, and Prudence turned her attention back to her cousin. "Oh, Anne, I wish I could speak to you now. I would tell you that, although I am every type of numbskull, I still feel as strongly for him as I ever did. Please wake up and tell me I am a buffoon, for there is no one else I have been honest with."

*

After spending another three days near to Anne, Fitzwilliam decided that, after an early morning visit to Anne, he would venture out to the mill. He had felt confined over the last few days. Prudence remained with Anne during the day, and things were still distant between them, and although he had explored the area on foot and on horseback, he had not travelled far, feeling guilty at being too far away from Anne.

Finally accepting that things were not going to change in the short term, he came to the conclusion that a trip to the mill would probably do him good. He travelled in the carriage with Mr. Huxley and Mr. Bamber. The tension had eased a little between himself and Mr. Huxley. Giving the steward credit for giving loyal service to his aunt and understanding the way his aunt reacted, plus his own unrequited feelings, led him to be more understanding after his initial anger had abated.

Fitzwilliam had never seen anything like it when they traversed the streets of Manchester. Yes, he lived in London, but for the most part, he remained in the areas frequented by the *ton*. This was different than what he had seen in the city. The streets leading into the centre became more built up and crowded the closer they got.

Terraced houses led off from the main road, and looking down the streets, he saw houses that seemed crowded somehow; they almost looked as if they were clambering to get on top of each other. Mills filled the skyline, their bulking angular masses seeming to block out the light. Smoke pumped from what seemed like thousands of chimneys, making Fitzwilliam wonder if there was any sunlight, and if there was, if it would ever reach the ground.

After watching as the carriage moved through the busy thoroughfare, he eventually sat back in wonderment and awe.

"It's a little different than what you are used to, I think," Mr. Bamber said with a grin at the stunned expression on the young man's face.

"Yes. I have never seen anything like it. It almost feels as if the buildings are closing in on us," Fitzwilliam admitted.

"This is the oldest area of the city. Thought I would bring you through this part, and then you can see the improvements we have made."

"He likes to shock our delicate sensibilities," Mr. Huxley said. He had been extremely quiet around Colonel Fitzwilliam since his arrival, but it was not through fear. He was determined to stand by Anne but knew he was powerless to help her whilst she was in such a precarious situation.

Mr. Bamber laughed. "I have to take my enjoyment from somewhere, and you were not half as shocked as the young Colonel here. You took it in your stride, my boy." As both Mr. Huxley and Colonel Fitzwilliam were above the age of thirty, they exchanged an amused look that the older gentleman still considered them boys.

"Did you inherit a mill?" Colonel Fitzwilliam asked.

"No. I worked my business up from scratch. My father was a cotton worker, but that wasn't going to be enough for me. The ability to work hard, learn quickly, and take a few risks meant that, when I met my lovely wife-to-be, I was a joint partner in my first mill. I soon branched out after we had wed and built my own. I was in the process of building the second when my lovely Charlotte died. I think I would have gone insane if it hadn't been for little Prudence and the two mills."

"I am surprised the family were so against the marriage if you were already successful," Fitzwilliam said.

Laughing, Mr. Bamber shook his head at Fitzwilliam. "They didn't want my tarnished credentials anywhere near their titled daughter. I suppose I cannot blame them. Now I am a man with a daughter myself, I can understand why they only wanted the best for Charlotte. I only want the best for Prudence, but that does not mean I'm foolish enough to want her to have a title."

"She did mention you were hoping for a viscount," Fitzwilliam could not resist pointing out.

"That was naught but a joke between father and daughter. I had already decided as long as she was happy, I would accept any man she chose. Unfortunately, she has not

153

wished to marry any of the gentlemen who have offered for her."

"She's had many offers?" Fitzwilliam asked.

Mr. Bamber noticed the strangled tone Fitzwilliam failed to hide when he spoke, and it pleased him. It seemed his daughter's chosen one was not as unaffected by her as he had first presumed. He would enjoy finding out more about the young man as he had already noticed how his eyes followed Prudence, especially when she hadn't realised she was being observed. There was a longing in Fitzwilliam's gaze that Prudence might not have noticed, but her father certainly had.

"Under ten but above five." He grinned. "She has a lot to offer, and the fact that she's a capable lass has only added to her appeal. A mill owner can't go far wrong if he has a capable helpmate by his side."

"I imagine not." Fitzwilliam was devastated. He had lost hope after Darcy's interference, but to be told that rich men sought the one he was still in love with had struck him as hard as if it had been a physical blow. He had little to offer her; he knew that, but to have it confirmed shattered the tiny fragment of hope he was clinging onto. His day had gone a little darker.

On arrival at the Bamber Mill, the three gentlemen alighted from the carriage. Fitzwilliam looked around. There was more space between the mill and houses than the others he had seen, but only slightly. The streets were about half the width of the streets he frequented in London, and yet there seemed to be about double the amount of traffic on them. Public houses and shops seemed to be on each street corner, with the residential houses spanning away in rigid lines of dark brick. A few people idly watched their arrival; they appeared to be older women, or women with

154

babes in arms. One or two were scrubbing the front steps or cleaning windows. It was clear they noticed the carriage but weren't interested enough in its occupants to stop their endeavours.

Mr. Bamber led the way through the bustling mill yard. Piles of products, from raw goods to boxes of finished items were stacked around the busy space. Mr. Bamber's arrival in the yard was noticed, the men doffing their caps and the women calling out good morning to him. A few of the woman cat-called or whistled at Mr. Huxley and Fitzwilliam.

Mr. Huxley glanced at Fitzwilliam. "If Mr. Bamber wasn't with us their calls would be far more raucous. I can say this with the voice of experience. It is terrifying."

"They are good workers, but they don't miss an opportunity to heckle," Mr. Bamber said. "They would frighten most men."

"We should have used them against the French," Fitzwilliam said.

"It would have been over a lot quicker if we had. No disrespect to you all, of course, but I've seen these girls in action. It's a shame what they put a callow youth through on his first day at work. He has to toughen up and fast if he is to survive their taunts." Mr. Bamber shuddered.

"No offence taken at your comparison. I am already afraid of walking through this yard unescorted. How does Miss Bamber deal with them?"

"Oh, Prudence is treated with affection by them all, but they can and do tease her," Mr. Bamber said. "She grew up around here, and a motherless child will always bring out the maternal streak in these girls. She was petted as a young girl, spoiled even."

Fitzwilliam was amazed as he walked through the cotton-filled loom room and card room. The noise was unbelievable as the large machinery whirred and clanked in place, with workers moving in time to the mechanical dance. The cotton fibres made him choke, but he noticed large fans moving the white snow away from the workers and machinery.

He was stunned for a moment or two when the door to the office closed and the noise was muted somewhat.

"It is an impressive sight at first look isn't it?" Mr. Huxley asked. "I was completely overawed."

"I have never seen anything like it," Fitzwilliam said.

"It warms my heart every time I walk through," Mr. Bamber admitted. "I'll never tire of the noise or the smell of the oil and cotton. However strange that sounds."

"It just makes you sound like a man happy with his lot in life," Fitzwilliam said.

"The only way to be. Why hanker after something we can't achieve? I would never be accepted in your circles, even though I could buy and sell most of those who would look down their noses at my humble beginnings. Who are the fools in that situation?"

"You make a good point, sir."

"Well I didn't bring you here to start talking about the rights and wrongs of society. Come, Mr. Huxley, let's show the Colonel what a working man's day is like!"

They were half-way through the afternoon when a breathless Prudence burst into the office, animated and flushed. Fitzwilliam had been pouring over some paperwork but immediately moved towards her.

"Anne?" he asked.

"Yes! She woke! Only for a little time, but she opened her eyes. The doctor says the fever has broken!"

"Oh, thank God!" Mr. Huxley exclaimed, sinking into a chair.

Fitzwilliam walked over to Prudence and squeezed her outstretched hands. "Thank you for all you have done. Thank you most sincerely."

Prudence returned the pressure of his fingers. "She managed to fight it. We didn't think she would, but she is stronger than we all thought. The doctor says there is still a long way to go before she is completely out of danger, but it's a start. I had to come tell you."

"We owe you a real debt of gratitude."

"I love Anne. Almost from the first moment I met her," Prudence admitted. Her hands were still grasped in Fitzwilliam's, and she made no effort to remove them.

"You brought out the best in her."

"I think two of us did," Prudence said, turning to Mr. Huxley. "Her journey north proves how smitten she is with you."

Fitzwilliam stiffened and took a step away from Prudence. He felt the loss of touching her but needed to dampen down what she was hinting at. "She could have been travelling to you," he said to Prudence.

"She told Mr. Huxley to come here. She followed him. Yes, she knew she would find a welcome here, but it was not us she was seeking."

Fitzwilliam looked as if to answer back but instead he turned to Mr. Bamber. "Do you wish me to leave immediately, sir, or am I able to remain until Anne shows further progress?"

"You can stay as long as you wish," Mr. Bamber said. "I shall leave it up to you to make the decision. You will find no push from me to rid us of your company. It's only natural you'd want to remain close by for a time."

157

"Thank you for your continued hospitality. I would like to make sure Anne is stronger before leaving her," Fitzwilliam said.

"Why don't you two accompany Prudence home? I am hardly likely to get any sense out of you for the rest of the day now that you know Miss Anne is improved," Mr. Bamber said.

As both men were indeed thinking about Anne, they jumped at the chance. Prudence led the way through the factory, acknowledging people as she went. There was no conversation as the noise was too great. Once in the yard their presence caused the same amount of interest as it had when the men had arrived.

"Oooh, Miss Prudence! Found yourself two fine gentlemen, have you? I don't mind taking one off your hands!" came a cackling cat-call.

"Now, Mary, your Joseph won't like that, but I will have either of those two," another responded. "A fine pair. Fancy walking out with a girl who knows how to look after a man, my lovelies? We'll not be prim and proper, I promise!"

Prudence choked on a laugh as Mr. Huxley and Fitzwilliam both looked abashed.

"Sally, you're putting them to the blush! Stop your teasing," Prudence chided.

"I ain't teasing, Miss Prudence. We don't often get fine fellows like those two visiting us. I am more than happy to give either of them a friendly welcome."

"I shall inform Brendon when I next see him, shall I?"

"Ooh, getting territorial, Miss Prudence? Well I can't blame you. Which one will you choose, or are you yet to make a decision?"

"I am not decided as yet," Prudence said with a laugh.

"Good on you, girl!" The women laughed and cheered good-naturedly, which although Prudence flushed, she smiled along with them.

Leaving the mill yard, Fitzwilliam sighed. "I did not think we would get out unmauled. They make the women who follow the drum look positively meek and mild."

"There's no harm in them," Prudence assured him.

"Not for you, but for a handsome beast like me..."

Prudence snorted. "Deluded man."

"But they just pointed out how fine I am. How can you go against those astute women?"

"They say exactly the same to the coal merchant, the waggon boys, and anyone else who has the misfortune of crossing the yard whilst they are outside."

"I am no better than a waggon boy?"

"Take comfort. She said you were on equal terms," Mr. Huxley pointed out.

"In that case, I am reassured," Fitzwilliam said as he climbed into the waiting carriage.

Chapter 17

Anne was still sleeping when the threesome arrived back in Stretford. There was a difference though. It was a natural slumber rather than an unconscious fever. Prudence took up her daily roll of nursemaid on her return and settled in for the afternoon.

Fitzwilliam joined her for a little while. They sat in silence, both watching Anne, but aware of every movement the other made. The atmosphere was not uncomfortable exactly, but there was an unresolved air to it.

After an hour, Prudence leaned forward in her seat. "Anne?" she whispered as a reaction to her cousin's eyes fluttering slightly.

Both waited, watching and willing the young woman in the bed to awaken. Eventually, she obliged them with a blink and then opened her eyes.

"Prudence?" she croaked.

"Yes, I am here, my dear. Would you like a drop of water?"

Anne nodded slightly, but they could both see that the movement cost her. Prudence wet a cloth and squeezed a drop or two onto the dry, parched lips. "A little at a time," she soothed when it seemed Anne would ask for more.

Fitzwilliam moved to the other side of his cousin's bed. Touching Anne's hand he smiled down at her when she looked at him. "Hello, sweetheart. It is so good to see you awake."

"Mother?" Anne croaked.

"She is well. As demanding as usual, I am led to believe," Fitzwilliam reassured her.

Anne smiled slightly. "M-Mr. Huxley?"

"He's here," Fitzwilliam said. "You must not worry about anything, Anne. The important thing is that you need to get better."

"Yes," Anne whispered. "Mr. Huxley."

"I promise you shall see him the next time you awaken, but I can see you are very tired. Sleep now," Prudence said.

Anne did not argue, but let her eyelids close and was soon breathing deeply.

Fitzwilliam watched her for a few minutes before he walked to the window and blindly looked out. Prudence left him a while but eventually his tense stance removed her inner battle with herself to remain at a distance from him.

Walking over to where he stood she rested a hand on his arm. "What troubles you?"

"I am terrified she will relapse," he admitted, not looking at Prudence.

"She is over the worst. I know there is still a long way to go before she will be fully recovered, but she has overcome the first hurdle. Have faith."

"It has only just struck me, but it has done so quite forcefully, that if Anne died, she has little experience of life. The restrictions she's faced have meant she has not had a season, nor a trip abroad. She has barely been to any entertainments, all because of my aunt's selfishness."

"There was probably some fear on our aunt's part," Prudence said.

"What? That Anne would find a life without her?"

"Possibly. It is not something to completely condemn our aunt for. Think of it from Aunt Catherine's perspective. Anne is all she has."

"It's the same with you and your father, but he hasn't restricted your life."

"No, he has not. But he has a business in which he can lose himself. Plus, I have always promised I would remain close by him. He knows I will live nearby, whereas Anne could have married someone and moved to the other end of the country," Prudence admitted.

"Is that why you refused the offers of marriage you have received?" Fitzwilliam was torturing himself. He knew that, but it did not stop him uttering the words. He inwardly cursed when Prudence removed her hand from his arm.

"Not that it is any of your business, but no. That was not the reason I refused the offers I received," came the cool response.

"I am sorry for asking."

"You should be."

"The reason for my impertinence is that I can think of little else other than what we shared and what I felt when I was with you. I will always damn my family to the devil for their interference."

Prudence sighed and walked away from Fitzwilliam. "This is not the time nor the place to go over old ground. Thinking about what happened since my return home, I have come to the conclusion that we would not have suited anyway. Oh, there is an attraction between us. I am not trying to deny that, but there needs to be more. I can barely explain what I mean, but perhaps it is summed up by my wishing for a husband to want me above everything else and put me first when it really matters. I have not yet found a man who would be prepared to do that."

"I am sorry that you feel that way. If it helps with your annoyance towards me, things will never be the same between myself and Darcy."

"That does not please me, believe me. It is not my hope that I would come between you and your family, but it is something between the two of you. It does not affect me, so do not remain estranged on my account."

"I think of you constantly."

Prudence closed her eyes. It would be so easy to go to him, to let him wrap her in his arms as he had done at Rosings. It was what she wanted. Unfortunately, her inner voice stopped her from acting though her heart wanted to capitulate. How could she risk his lack of support when they would start with his family clearly against the match? No. To face such censure as they would, the pair had to be completely in tune with each other, just as her parents had been. Fitzwilliam had shown that he was not that committed to her.

"I am going to inform Mr. Huxley that Anne has been awake and invite him to sit with me. It is clear that Anne wishes to see him, and I think it's only fair that we abide by her wishes," she said dully.

"As you wish," Fitzwilliam answered. He moved to the door. "Let me send him up to you."

Prudence sank into her chair when Fitzwilliam bowed and left the room. Blowing out her cheeks, she looked at Anne, who was still sleeping. "I cannot arrange my own happy ever after, for common sense will not let me, but I can certainly try and help yours," she said.

*

The evening meal was a less tense affair than it had been over the previous evenings. Mr. Bamber, as usual, had asked of Anne's progress.

"She is waking regularly and looking brighter each time," Prudence said, tucking into the veal pie, which was nearest to her.

"That is good. The fresh air here will do her good once she's up and about."

"I should make arrangements for her removal as soon as possible," Fitzwilliam said.

"I doubt she will be fit to travel for some time yet," Prudence said quickly. "She would not be able to stand a relapse."

"That would mean we shall be imposing on you for quite a while. We are already trespassing on you a great deal."

"It is not intruding in any way," Mr. Bamber said. "She is family. She stays for as long as is needed and beyond if she so wishes."

"Thank you."

"It is no trouble, and I know Prudence will enjoy a bit of female company around the place. She spends too much time in the presence of my cronies rather than people her own age."

"As our closest neighbour in age is Selina, I can do without female company, thank you very much. She only speaks if it is to have a dig at something or someone," Prudence said.

"I'm surprised you haven't put her in her place. You were an expert with Lady Catherine, and half the time, she didn't realise what you were doing," Fitzwilliam said.

Prudence laughed at him. "That's outrageous! I did nothing of the sort!"

"She did," Fitzwilliam said to Mr. Bamber, enjoying the response his words had caused. It was the first time her eyes had sparkled at him, and although it had increased the ache of longing in his chest, he was glad to see her old playfulness return.

"Talking of your aunt," Mr. Bamber stated, "she needs to be made to come round to the idea of the joining of Miss Anne and this young man," he said nodding in Mr. Huxley's direction.

"Why?" Fitzwilliam asked, all laughter gone.

"Come. You must see your cousin's situation? You cannot have forgotten this all started because they were found together."

Fitzwilliam frowned at Mr. Huxley. "Lady Catherine would never countenance a marriage to you."

"I know that," Mr. Huxley responded.

"Yet you behaved inappropriately."

"To my shame, I did. I would defy any man who is truly in love to be able to resist kissing the one he cares for above all others."

Fitzwilliam flushed at Mr. Huxley's words, but did not stop glaring at the younger man.

Mr. Bamber had watched the interchange with amusement but thought it prudent to intervene. "It seems that your aunt has little choice about what she will and will not accept. If the girl was compromised, and it is public knowledge, then there's little to be done except arrange an early marriage."

"She still has a long way to go with her recovery yet," Fitzwilliam pointed out.

"You'd rather her have a relapse or even die than make an imprudent match?" Mr. Bamber asked with interest.

"No! Not at all! I am just pointing out that we have jumped from celebrating her consciousness to marrying her. It seems a little premature."

"Might as well start planning for that, young man. For if I know anything, as sure as the sun will rise in the morning and set at night, if there is chance for gossip from a family who does everything to avoid it, the tittle-tattlers will take exceptional pleasure from spreading rumours," Mr. Bamber said.

Fitzwilliam rubbed his hands over his face in despair. "You are perfectly correct. There are many whom Lady Catherine has upset in some way or another. They will take great joy in this situation."

"Then you had best start a plan to limit the damage to that poor girl. She could do a lot worse than Huxley here. He's a hard worker and an intelligent lad."

"I doubt those are factors Lady Catherine will consider as benefits," Fitzwilliam responded dryly.

"She thought them important when he was looking after her estate. That must be just as important as her daughter is to her," Mr. Bamber shrugged.

"Papa!" Prudence could not stop the laugh from escaping.

Looking unrepentant, Mr. Bamber smiled at his daughter. "She sounds just like her parents. Can't see what's good for her daughter even though it is as obvious as the nose on her face. If Miss Anne loves him and will be happy, all the rest is irrelevant. I would say Rosings would be in the best of hands if Huxley is to continue looking after it. It seems a no-nonsense solution to everything. I have no idea why there will be so much fuss. Lady Catherine clearly did not learn from the experience with her sister."

"To be fair, sir, you were and are far richer than I ever will be. There are justifiable objections to my suit," Mr. Huxley said. He might be wishing to marry Anne, but he was fully aware of his shortcomings.

"But you bring skill and experience, and you love Miss Anne. Do not put yourself down, lad. There are plenty who will do that for you. Don't be quick to give them the tools to beat you with," Mr. Bamber responded.

Mr. Huxley flushed but smiled gratefully at Mr. Bamber. "Thank you, sir."

"I think you will be a good husband to Miss Anne."

"Papa, you really need to start giving Anne her title. She is Lady Anne," Prudence gently scolded.

"A title is nothing at the end of the day. It won't put food on the table, whereas this young man has worked for years on that estate, making sure it is profitable. That is what matters. Your mother was never concerned with her title, and Miss Anne shouldn't be either. Seems to me it brings nothing but unhappiness anyway."

"I doubt Lady Catherine would agree," Fitzwilliam said.

"And that is precisely why her daughter is in the predicament she is in now. Her mother could have avoided scandal and gossip, but we are where we are. So, Colonel Fitzwilliam, I suggest you persuade your aunt, so that when Miss Anne is well enough she can be married by special licence."

"Dear Lord! I will not look forward to that conversation!" Fitzwilliam said with a grimace.

"Coward," Prudence muttered.

Fitzwilliam shot her a look tinged with amusement. "Would you like to have the conversation in my place?"

"Not at all, but I do wish I could be there to hear it," Prudence said. "Sorry, Mr. Huxley. My funning is aimed at Aunt Catherine's foolishness. I think you perfectly suited to my cousin. I always did."

"I suspected as much when you arranged for me to take the reins on the carriage ride through the grounds," Mr. Huxley said.

"Yes. She was obvious and playing a dangerous game, which I warned her about," Fitzwilliam said.

"I regret that the situation has come to Anne fighting through a terrible illness, but I know how much Anne thought of Mr. Huxley from the start. Ladies do not have secrets. They often declare their innermost feelings to one another," Prudence said. "I was fully aware that she had a tendrè for Mr. Huxley, and it was clear he felt the same."

The young man blushed at receiving so much attention and having his supposed hidden feelings so easily interpreted. "I will do anything I can to make Lady Anne happy."

"That is all a mother and her family should wish for a young girl," Mr. Bamber said with a pointed look at Fitzwilliam. "You have a task ahead of you, but before you leave us, I advise you to let Prudence take you for a drive tomorrow through the parkland near the river."

"I shall be sitting with Anne," Prudence said quickly.

"I think you can hand that role over to her future husband," Mr. Bamber said.

"But you will need me at the mill, sir. I would not wish to shirk my duty. I have already worked a short day today," Mr. Huxley said.

"You will be more use here. Prudence needs some fresh air. She hasn't been out properly for days. I did not say anything when Miss Anne was suffering from the fever, but as a parent, it is my job to look after my girl, and she needs a break from the sick room," Mr. Bamber said.

"I would like to see a little of the green spaces around here," Fitzwilliam said. He was loath to give up any opportunity of spending time with Prudence. "I haven't strayed very far from the house when out on my own."

"It would be my pleasure to show you a little of Stretford," Prudence said, but the look she shot her father spoke volumes that politeness prevented her words doing.

Chapter 18

Fitzwilliam handed Prudence into the gig they were to take out. It was pulled by two fine-looking chestnuts that Prudence had made a fuss of when she left the house. Settling onto the seat, she handed the reins to Fitzwilliam when he climbed nimbly onto his side.

"Really?" he asked in surprise.

"I know what you cavalry officers are like, remember? I shall direct, but you may drive," Prudence said.

"I was looking forward to sitting back and criticising," Fitzwilliam admitted.

"Brute. Fortunately for me, I am one step ahead of you!"

"Always, it would seem."

They drove in silence for a while, enjoying being outside. Prudence pointed out sites of interest, but both were fully aware of wishing to enjoy their time together. Eventually they came to a halt at the river side.

"I admit I did not expect to see such a beautiful area after travelling into the city centre when I visited the mills. It's like a different world, yet it is so close," Fitzwilliam said.

"You haven't seen the city in one of the fogs or the rain. It can be very bleak, but here we do not get the same smog. Father says it is something to do with the wind direction caused by the Pennine Hills. I have no idea if that is true, but we do seem to be more sheltered here."

"It is lovely. I wish I had more time to explore the surrounding area. One thing this trip has taught me is that I need to explore this country a little more. I have seen more of the continent than I have of my own country, and I need to remedy that."

"You cannot be criticised about not exploring England when you were serving your King and country against Napoleon."

"No. I suppose not. It's strange. When I left Oxford, I was completely sure that the cavalry was the only thing I wanted to do. I had the urge to make a difference, to serve my country and be around the finest horseflesh at the same time. It suited me down to the ground. But these last few months have made me consider that it is perhaps time I was looking for another occupation."

"Really?" Prudence was stunned at his words and turned towards him. "I thought you loved the cavalry?"

"I do. Being on active duty and around my men and horses all day isn't like work for me. Oh, the battles are not pleasurable obviously, and the nightmares of those I suppose I will carry with me forever. But does it make sense to say everything aside from the active service is like being a part of one large, welcoming family? Even then, we are working together to try to keep each other alive as well as ourselves," Fitzwilliam explained.

"I can understand the feelings of belonging. I thought I could fit in anywhere. Arrogant of me, I know," Prudence said. "But being at Rosings showed me that my home is around these parts, and there are areas of society in which I would not be comfortable. I admit the realisation took me aback a little."

It was Fitzwilliam's turn to look surprised. "You seemed perfectly comfortable even though you were treated so ill. In fact, I never once thought you appeared out of place."

"I was treated like a member of staff, and Lady Catherine would point out that it was no surprise that I seemed to fit in!" Prudence said. "If that was my being treated ill, surely it means the poor companion who I replaced is also treated poorly?"

"I think she probably is. Something else we have to be ashamed of — that we stood by and let the poor woman be put through goodness knows what by our aunt."

"Your — our — family is likely not very different from many others of the aristocracy," Prudence said.

"It does not make it right though, does it? I know I for one will be reflecting on my behaviour towards others in the future."

Prudence smiled at him. "Our aunt will be accusing you of being influenced by the working masses."

"We could take a leaf out of their book. Talking of my aunt, I have been thinking I should depart tomorrow. I need to call on Darcy to inform him of what has been happening and what needs to take place and then return to Rosings. It won't be an easy task persuading Aunt Catherine what is best for Anne," Fitzwilliam said. "I will also be telling her that she should remain at Rosings and not travel. I think Anne would recover quicker and more beneficially without Aunt Catherine fussing or demanding around her."

"That is between you and her. If she does decide to travel, she will be made welcome here."

"You are very good."

"Not at all. I would do anything for Anne."

"Anything?"

"I do not like the look of speculation in your expression, Fitzwilliam," Prudence said.

"It's just that Anne would like to see me happy...
and..."

Prudence flushed, but could not resist his teasing
tone. "As much as I think I shall regret asking this: And?"

Fitzwilliam laughed gently. "And what would make
me very happy would be the thought that one day — one
day — however far away that might be, you might consider
giving me a second chance."

"My fortune has made me worth the effort of going
against the family?" Prudence could not help the bitterness
in her voice, and she moved to turn away from him.

Fitzwilliam reached out and took hold of her cheek,
gently forcing her to look at him. "No. This has nothing to do
with money, but everything to do with the fact that I have
not had a decent night's sleep since you left Rosings. I feel
guilty because the first thought I had when I received
Darcy's express was not about Anne who was close to death,
but by having a reason to travel here, I would get to see you
again. What kind of cad does that make me? And I want to
delay my removal until I can work out a way that will
convince you to give me that second chance, but I know I
owe it to Anne to help with her future happiness."

Prudence blinked at the heartfelt words. She started
to speak but had to swallow an unexpected lump in her
throat.

"Have I said too much? Are you going to cast me out
of the gig?" Fitzwilliam asked. For once all his natural
laughter was gone. He was as serious as she had ever seen
him.

Prudence could not resist the appeal in his voice or
the way he was trying to be confident, but his eyes betrayed
the uncertainty his bravado hid. "No. I am not going to make

you walk back, however tempting that would be. Not because of your words, just to be cruel."

"Wretch."

"Fitzwilliam, I am afraid to trust what you say," she said. "I have had offers in the past, but they have been made mainly because of my fortune."

"But you are beautiful!"

"I am taller than some men, and I speak my mind. I accept that I am not an ape-leader, but there are far prettier girls out there who have better figures and are more amenable. My idiosyncrasies are accepted because of what I inherit."

"But I fell in love with you before I knew any of that. Well, I did know you spoke your mind. I knew that within moments of meeting you, but I had no idea of your background."

"You say you love me, but you did not offer marriage when we were together. When we exchanged kisses. Many kisses. In fact you withdrew impressively when I mentioned that we could be caught and forced to marry," Prudence pointed out.

Fitzwilliam turned to face the front of the gig. The horses were becoming restless, but this was important. He felt if this weren't sorted between them, his chance to secure her would be gone forever. "I am a fool. I know without doubt I am. You have to understand something about me. I have spent most of my life in the shadow of my brother, who I love dearly, and Darcy, who I don't love quite as much since his interference between us, but I used to. They have money and looks. I am not a handsome devil, although I have been told I have an engaging address."

"You do."

"Thank you." He smiled despite the seriousness of the situation he was facing. "In my society, the second son is always overlooked. We are never rich enough nor handsome enough to tempt the debutantes. Now, I am not saying this for pity. It is the truth. I think I did not take what was happening between us as seriously as it was becoming to me because I was conditioned into believing that I needed a rich wife, and that was what I was going to get."

"You told me that's what you needed."

"Yes. The thing is, the more I got to know you, the less important that seemed. I struggled with trying to work out how we could live on my income, which doesn't cover all my expenses, and I rely on the kindness of family members to supplement it. Do you know how demeaning and insecure that can make a person feel?"

"No. I suppose not."

"I belong to a loving family, and I love my occupation, but if I wanted to marry you, I had to work out how I could achieve that in realistic terms. In most moments I just thought to heck with it. If we married, we would find a way around it, but life isn't that easy when there is no money. I did not want you to suffer as a consequence. For I would hate to make you unhappy because I could not provide a good lifestyle for you. Then Darcy arrived."

"Yes. He did."

"He is a good man," Fitzwilliam defended his cousin. "He's been like my own brother and has been father and brother to his own sister who lost her parents when she was very young. I respect him and his opinions. Unfortunately, he repeated aloud what I had been struggling with internally. It wouldn't have been too bad, but he uttered the words before I had managed to work out a solution in my own mind. I was faced with the nightmare situation in which we found ourselves. I admit I just panicked and could not think straight."

"I felt attacked."

"I am so sorry that I did not respond as I should have done. I truly am."

"I believe you. I think."

"I suppose that is a start. I hate to say this, but if we don't move soon, I think the horses will bolt," Fitzwilliam said reluctantly.

"We have been gone some time. We should be heading home."

"Cousin — Prudence, please consider allowing us to have that second chance. I do not think either of us will be happy if we don't."

Prudence looked away for a few moments, and Fitzwilliam took the reins and started the journey back to the house. He had done all he could. If she still did not want him, there was nothing else he could do to persuade her.

Before they left the parkland, Prudence turned to face Fitzwilliam. "Come back after all this has been sorted out between Mr. Huxley and Anne. Wait until the dust has settled on that and then come for a visit. Let us get to know each other again. From the start, but with honesty on both sides. I, too, was at fault. I should have been truthful about my situation."

"It wouldn't have made any difference. There would still have been prejudice about where your fortune came from. Certainly in my aunt's case."

"Luckily for us, she is an aunt not a parent, and I now understand how the family dynamics have worked until now."

Fitzwilliam smiled. "So I can return?"

"Yes."

"It might be a little while. Aunt Catherine isn't going to be persuaded easily."

"I can wait."

"I am not sure if I can."

"Do not push your advantage."

Laughing Fitzwilliam kissed her gloved hand. "You cannot blame a man for trying."

Chapter 19

If Colonel Fitzwilliam thought he would spend a day or two at Rosings and then head north once more, he was to be disappointed. Aunt Catherine was furious that Anne was not with him when he returned, and after her hysterics had calmed on hearing how ill Anne was, she would not countenance a marriage between her daughter and Mr. Huxley.

"Never! As long as I have breath in my body, I shall never approve of such a match."

"She is of age."

"I shall disinherit her! Unless she returns to me. Unwed."

"Then she shall be ruined in the eyes of society," Fitzwilliam said.

"Nonsense! She is a De Bourgh! She will be nothing of the sort. No one would dare to believe rumours of one of my family."

"Are you sure about that, Aunt?" Fitzwilliam asked. "It is a heck of a risk to take with Anne's reputation. As the situation stands at the moment, we can fudge over the reality of what actually happened. Her illness can be made public, saying that she became ill when visiting her cousin Prudence, but then happened to fall in love with Mr. Huxley. It is a surprising match, but one that you approve of because your wish is for your daughter to be happy."

"Do not be ridiculous! As if I would lower myself to repeat such a Banbury tale!"

"I hope Anne is able to withstand the cuts she will receive in society. And you as a consequence."

"Why would I be affected?"

"Anne lives here. No one will visit a family in which a ruined girl still resides. Unless you wish to cast her off, of course, and send her to live somewhere else."

Lady Catherine rose from her chair and stormed across the room. "As if I would send Anne away to live elsewhere!"

"You have just threatened to disinherit her."

"She would return before I was forced to do that."

"That's fine, but I can't see Sir James visiting. How shocked would his mother be to know you had allowed Anne back into Rosings? You have been missing for days, and Anne has also been absent. What rumours and gossip are already circulating?"

"If I find out that any of the servants have been spreading rumours, they shall be cast off without a reference." Lady Catherine glared at the unfortunate footman, who stood guarding the door.

"The fact that you have already sent Mr. Huxley away will have convinced the servants of that. It will most certainly have been reported with wonder and speculation, particularly because you seemed to be perfectly happy with the last few years of Mr. Huxley's work."

"Damn the neighbourhood!"

"You should have been more circumspect, Aunt," Fitzwilliam said gently. "If you had not overreacted when the news reached you that Anne had been foolish, you would not be facing any of this now."

"So it is my fault, is it?" Lady Catherine demanded.

"No. Not as such, but your reaction to it was not prudent."

Lady Catherine looked at her nephew through narrowed eyes. "You have changed. You never used to be so objectionable."

Laughing, and with a shake of his head, Fitzwilliam indicated that his aunt should sit. "I was always the one who soothed you when Darcy told you the truth of a situation. That is all. I am having to play the role of Darcy in this situation."

"Yes. Because that woman is having yet another brat."

"Aunt, that is unfair. Darcy is the happiest we have ever seen him. Elizabeth is a perfect wife for him. You did not meet the women who fawned over him when he was single. Believe me, if he had married any of those, we would all have been sorry. He had a lucky escape when he did not fall for the so-called charms of the likes of Caroline Bingley," Fitzwilliam said of one of the women who had been determined to set her cap at Darcy.

Lady Catherine sat down at her nephew's request. "At least they would have come from the right stock."

"Aunt, you cannot, in all countenance, wish an unhappy marriage on someone you care for just because the man or woman in question comes from the right kind of family, surely?"

Lady Catherine narrowed her eyes at her nephew. "Is this to do with that girl who tried to insinuate herself with you?"

"If you are referring to your niece, Prudence, no it has nothing to do with her. This is about Anne, and if you are going to stand by your daughter. Are you, Aunt? Or are you happy to remain here alone and estranged?" Fitzwilliam had riled at his aunt's words, but had managed to keep his expression bland. She was being pig-headed and foolish, but he was aware that if the discussion turned into an argument, only Anne would suffer, for Lady Catherine would become even more belligerent.

"I would have to admit a steward into the front of the house. He would be in charge of Anne's fortune."

"This is not about money," Fitzwilliam ground out. "It is about Anne finding a man who loves her for all her fragility and who is a decent, hardworking man. He has already shown he is committed to Rosings and will work hard to protect and develop the estate."

"The ruination of Anne was probably his intention from the start."

"Aunt, that is unjust."

"What else am I to think?"

"That your daughter is loveable enough to fall in love with?"

Lady Catherine went silent for a while. Fitzwilliam thought he had struck a chord with his aunt, but then she looked at him, her expression full of disdain. "Love? Pah! That is for fools!" She stood and walked out of the room, flinging the words, "I shall hear no more of this!" over her shoulder as she went.

Fitzwilliam ground his teeth in frustration. He would have to stay longer than he wished. Yet again, his family was getting in the way of his happiness, and he cursed them for it.

*

Days.
It took days.

And still she would not agree.

Fitzwilliam had never been as vexed in his life, trying different arguments that would persuade his aunt's unyielding stance on the fate of her daughter.

He was eventually to receive support from an unexpected source — Mr. Collins.

When Lady Catherine had no company, she invited the clergyman around far more than she did when she was being entertained. Normally, if Darcy and Fitzwilliam were visiting, Mr. Collins would receive only one or two invitations. On this visit though, Lady Catherine did not wish to spend time with Fitzwilliam; his challenges were unwelcome to a woman who expected her word to be final. She had never seen this pugnacious side of her nephew, and she did not like it.

As a result, Mr. Collins was invited at some point every day. This added to Fitzwilliam's frustration as the man was an overt sycophant where his aunt was concerned, and it did not do his cause any good when Mr. Collins supported Lady Catherine whenever she spoke.

On the sixth day of Fitzwilliam's return to Rosings he entered the large grandiose drawing room. Lady Catherine was seated, resplendent on her favourite sofa, the folds of her heavily embroidered dress clashing harshly with the busy fabric on the piece of furniture. Mr. Collins in his clergy garb sat opposite Lady Catherine, leaning towards her in an almost seated bow.

Sighing silently, Fitzwilliam acknowledged Mr. Collins with a nod before helping himself to a brandy. Tea was available on the table next to Lady Catherine, but Fitzwilliam was finding more and more that tea did not remove the tension like brandy did when sitting in a room with the two characters he now faced.

"Have you heard from Manchester today?" Lady Catherine demanded as she did every time she first saw Fitzwilliam. He had been out on a ride during the morning to try to clear his head for the afternoon he would spend trying to persuade his aunt into accepting the fact that Anne had to be married.

"I have. Anne continues to make progress, albeit very slowly. She is staying awake for more than an hour at a time now," Fitzwilliam said. His highlight of the day was receiving the letters that Prudence sent. Yes, they were all about Anne, but in the farewell paragraph she always expressed her desire to see him soon, which helped to lift his spirits.

"It is a blessing that Lady Anne is recovering," Mr. Collins stated. "But as Sir James was saying only last night, it is so difficult for yourself."

"How so?" Lady Catherine demanded.

"No longer being able to welcome her at Rosings. We were discussing last night how it must grieve you for it to be so."

Fitzwilliam sat back in his chair, taking a sip of his drink. The afternoon had suddenly become far more interesting if the expression on his aunt's face were anything to go by.

"And why would I turn my back on Anne? It is only that my own health has had a set-back in recent weeks that I am not by her side at this moment," Lady Catherine said.

"With her ruination being so publicly known, I am only even more convinced of your magnanimous nature that you would go to her if you were able. She must feel honoured that, even though she will never see Rosings again, she might be allowed to see you. For she must repine at the loss of her family and friends." Mr. Collins was blithely forging ahead, as always misreading the signs emanating from the person he was in conversation with.

"Anne shall be returning to Rosings the moment she is well enough to travel," Lady Catherine said.

"My dear madam, please allow me to offer my advice on this matter. I strongly advise you against such a course of action. The neighbourhood — "

"Are nothing to me!" Lady Catherine exploded. "How dare you? How dare you come into my home and tell me what I should and should not be doing? I have never heard anything so utterly offensive in my life!"

"Lady Ca—"

"Do. Not. Interrupt. Me. I shall be giving Sir James a piece of my mind, and if I see or hear of anything — a single word or a look out of place — I shall know how to act," Lady Catherine said.

"Lady Catherine, please. Think about this," Mr. Collins appealed.

"I want you out of my sight, you foolish man!" Lady Catherine responded. "But you can tell everyone that my daughter shall be returning to Rosings and taking her rightful place as the heiress to this estate. If anyone has an issue with that, I suggest they come and visit me. Now go! I cannot bear to be near you!"

Her words sent the unfortunate clergyman scuttling from the room whilst looking anxiously back at his patroness. The room fell into an uneasy silence for a few moments before Fitzwilliam broke the quiet.

"I don't know whether to pity or admire him."

"He is a fool."

"He's only repeating what is being discussed throughout the area."

"I will make sure it stops."

"You know full well, as a ruined woman, she would not receive a welcome here. The best course of action you can take is to minimise the damage." Fitzwilliam managed to suppress a smile at the glare his words caused. The fact that she was not cursing him to the devil as she had done every other time he had brought up the subject so far was, hopefully, a sign of progress.

"And I suppose you think a marriage to someone wholly inappropriate would improve matters?"

"Not in the short term. Aunt, Anne is going to take a long time to recover from this. She will be absent for some time. Why not send her somewhere to recuperate when she is strong enough to travel, rather than immediately returning to Rosings?" Fitzwilliam was thinking on the spur of the moment, but a plan was forming that he thought might work.

"Where?"

"Let her remain in Manchester, and you sort out someone to be a deputy steward, for I doubt Mr. Huxley will return without Anne, and I can't blame him." He had seen that she was about to argue and had spoken before she could interrupt. "Then take her to the continent for some warm, fresh air. She has never been abroad. Let her travel and recuperate."

"What happens with Huxley?"

"I think for Anne's sake, she should be married before she leaves Manchester, and he should travel with you."

"Preposterous!"

"Not at all. It would be easier for you to have a gentleman travelling with you. He is intelligent and capable. Anne will be happy with him by her side, and whilst you are away you can start to teach him how to be the gentleman."

Fitzwilliam felt a modicum of sympathy for what he was volunteering Huxley for, but better that than the man lose the woman he loved. "There would be no better teacher. When you return to the area, months will have passed, and other gossip will have lowered the interest in Anne's story, as it always does. I'm not saying there will not be some mutterings when you first return, but it will be temporary."

"You are speaking as if we shall be gone for some time."

"I think the longer the better. In the main for Anne's health, but also for the neighbourhood to have become bored with speculation."

"What if she gets with child?"

"What of it?"

"She might not survive." For the first time Lady Catherine looked vulnerable and unsure. Fitzwilliam had the suspicion that she had revealed the real reason she was so against Anne's marrying anyone.

Standing, he walked to his aunt and knelt before her, taking her hands in his. "Aunt, none of us knows what the future will bring, but please, speak to Huxley and Anne of your concerns. There are ways of stopping children if she would be in especial danger by becoming with child."

Lady Catherine looked uncomfortable at the tenderness she was being shown, but Fitzwilliam kept hold of her hands.

Eventually, she stood. "Send word that I consent to the marriage. I shall not travel north, but I expect that Huxley will make arrangements that, when Anne is well enough, we shall travel to the south of France for a twelve-month."

"It's the right thing to do. You will see."

"I suppose now you have managed to browbeat me into submission, you will be leaving?" Lady Catherine asked.

"I have been away from my regiment for quite a while," Fitzwilliam answered. "I hope to be travelling to Manchester soon, but I need to go to London first."

"You are going to marry Charlotte's girl, aren't you?" Lady Catherine mentioned her sister by name for the first time.

"I hope so, Aunt. I truly hope so."

"Neither you, Darcy, nor Anne have considered the purity of the family bloodlines."

"Perhaps not, but we will all be happy with the people we have chosen as husbands and wives and surely that is what matters?"

"I expect you will be spouting sonnets when we next meet!"

Fitzwilliam laughed. "I hope not! I don't wish to frighten Prudence away so early in our acquaintance. She would never agree to a marriage if she hears my bumbling attempts to be romantic with words. Give me a battlefield, and I know exactly what to do. Matters of the heart are a completely different situation to contend with."

"You managed to talk me around with your flowery words."

"Oh, I think that had more to do with Mr. Collins than my endeavours."

"It shall be a long time before I can face him again."

"Aunt, he is your biggest supporter after your own family." Fitzwilliam thought it prudent not to point out that Mr. Collins was probably the only one who hung on his aunt's every word. "Don't keep him away. You are going to need company over the coming weeks if you are to stay at

Rosings. Invite him back soon. You know he will spend the next half dozen meetings apologising to you."

"I thought things would return to normal. I even had a letter this morning from Mrs. Jenkinson saying that she was well enough to return to her role as Anne's companion. I suppose I won't need her now."

"You like Mrs. Jenkinson, don't you?"

"She is efficient enough and very obliging."

"Why don't you change her terms of employment? Ask her to be your companion."

"I will have Anne and Mr. Huxley."

"They will be newlywed. Surely you would not wish to be in their company all of the time? It might be an idea for you to have a companion who can do as you wish. That way you can please yourself more than if you were alone with Anne and Mr. Huxley."

"Your suggestion does have some merit," Lady Catherine admitted.

"Give Mrs. Jenkinson a pay rise as would befit her new position."

"That would be unnecessary."

"You do not wish for it to be known that you promote servants without suitable recompense, surely?"

Lady Catherine's ever-present glare ratcheted up a notch. "No."

"Perfect. That's settled then. I shall make arrangements to travel to London in the morning," Fitzwilliam said.

"I suppose you are very pleased with all your organising and interference in my life."

"Not at all. I shall hand that baton back to Darcy as soon as he is able to leave Pemberley once more. I find being the placating nephew a far easier prospect."

"Impudent pup!"

Chapter 20

Fitzwilliam travelled back to London after he had written to Darcy, Prudence, and Mr. Huxley, updating them of the progress he had made. He knew Anne would be happy, and although he had cursed Huxley to the devil, he understood completely what his motivation had been. He ached to see Prudence again and hoped that it would only be a few days before he set out once more for Manchester.

He had some thinking to do before his journey north. Prudence had made it quite clear that she wanted to remain near her father and her life in Manchester. He was based in London. He would have to speak to his senior officer about what his options were. He would happily resign his commission to be with Prudence, but that would take away his only form of income. He had tried to think of alternatives, but at the moment he had no choice other than to remain with his cavalry regiment.

Yes, Prudence was a wealthy heiress, but his pride would not allow him to offer for her when he had absolutely nothing to offer but himself. It was the only cloud on his otherwise hopeful horizon.

Arriving in London a few days after leaving his aunt, he strolled into the barracks, greeting fellow officers. Noticing that something was amiss, he sought out his commanding officer.

"Sir, has there been a resurgence of Boney? There are many men and horses missing," he asked.

"Not Boney, but there has been some unrest. We have deployed troops to help keep order in some of the towns and cities across the country. I could hardly believe that a poor harvest could result in rioting."

"Rioting? Whatever for?"

"It's all tied up with the blasted corn laws. Have you not been keeping abreast with the newspapers?"

"No. To be honest I haven't sat down with a newspaper for days. I have been dealing with a family crisis," Fitzwilliam said.

"Yes, you mentioned that's why you needed a leave of absence. Everything sorted now?"

"Yes. We have reached the point where my assistance is no longer required."

"Good. You will have little time to kick your heels if these disturbances carry on. We have just sent a unit to the north. Poor blighters, they won't be able to understand a word the locals say. It's like they speak a foreign language, I tell you."

"Where in the north?" Fitzwilliam's relaxed stance had disappeared. He knew almost without asking.

"Manchester. They went a few days ago. There has been a lot of unrest on the streets there recently. It seems to be getting worse by the day."

"Sir. I need you to send me there."

"What? No! You're not needed."

"Sir. I have family there. Involved with the mills. I need to check on their safety," Fitzwilliam said.

"Have you indeed? This family of yours has caused me a whole lot of problems recently."

"I apologise sir, but understand that I would not be asking lightly. I will ensure my presence will be useful and not a waste of your resources."

"It's highly irregular."

"I would not ask if I did not think it important, sir."

"If you must check on them, I suppose you should go. Family is important, although yours is becoming a damned nuisance."

"Thank you, sir. They would not intentionally cause problems, I assure you, but in this instance, I have concerns about their safety," Fitzwilliam said.

When dismissed, Fitzwilliam ran to his lodgings. He had never felt panic like it when he realised that Manchester was the focus of the problems. Hoping that Prudence was safe enough in Stretford, he quickly arranged with his batman what needed to be taken with them. Both used to travelling for active duty, they were soon on the road again.

For Fitzwilliam, it was going to be a long journey.

*

Prudence hurried down the street towards her father's second mill. It was a journey she must have done a thousand times, but today it felt different.

There was a tension in the air that had never been there previously, and she was consciously aware of everything and everyone around her. Breathing a sigh of relief when she reached the mill yard, she hurried across the flagged space to the main mill building.

Entering her father's office, she took off her gloves and closed the door behind her, remaining dressed in the rest of her outerwear.

"Papa, you need to return home. We need to leave."

Mr. Bamber looked up. "I thought you would stay at home today. I told you how it has been lately," he scolded gently.

"I should have listened to you more. I did not imagine quite how the atmosphere has changed. Although it does make my journey even more important as I wanted to make sure you were safe and to persuade you for once to leave the mill early," Prudence explained.

"It is safe inside the mill. No one would breach the gates."

"You don't know that, Papa. I have never felt anything like what is currently swirling out there, and it's nothing to do with the fog that is starting to descend."

"I am not going to get any peace until I give in and come home, am I?"

"No," Prudence said. She pulled on her gloves and tightened the ribbon on her bonnet. "Can we leave immediately?"

"I suppose I must," Mr. Bamber said. He reluctantly pushed the chair away from the table and took his greatcoat from the hook on the back of the closed door.

Prudence helped her father fasten his coat and kissed his cheek. "Thank you. I could not settle at home with you still here."

"Fusspot."

"I do not apologise for it," Prudence said, completely unrepentant. "You are more precious to me than anyone else, and I would like to keep you safe."

"What? I rank above a certain young cavalry officer? I think you are funning with me. I refuse to believe I rate so high."

Laughing, Prudence took her father's arm. "You are a beast. Fine. I admit you are equal. Is that better?"

"Most certainly. I never had you down for a girl prone to Banbury tales. Now let us get home and spend some time with Miss Anne."

Prudence shook her head at her father. He never gave Anne her title, but it was not done out of rudeness; he was already very fond of her and spent a while visiting her each day. Anne had been embarrassed and shy at first with the uncle she had never met, but it wasn't very long before Mr. Bamber had charmed her.

Anne was still far from fully recovered, but each day she was spending more time awake, and although not yet ready to leave her bed, she could sit up and speak for an hour at a time without needing to rest.

Prudence let Mr. Huxley spend as much time with Anne as he could. Mr. Bamber had not pursued the fact that Mr. Huxley was supposed to be working for him now. They had all been convinced that one way or another he would marry Anne and as a result have no need for a reference.

Climbing into the carriage, which had been brought out of the stable yard in the mill, Prudence looked around her, not in fear so much as wariness. "I've never felt an unease like it," she admitted.

"No. The poor harvest has driven prices up to ridiculous levels. I can't employ any more than I do already, but there are soldiers and sailors aplenty no longer needed and desperate for work, which just is not there," Mr. Bamber said. He was unusually serious. "We have been pushing for some support from the government, but all they are bothered about is themselves and their aristocratic friends. The poor labourers who are soon going to be starving to death are of little consequence."

"Can we do nothing to help?"

"I am employing more than I should and keeping wages at a reasonable level, although many of my fellow owners have reduced wages. I am trying to work out how to feed the workers during the day, so that at least they will have full bellies whilst they're working. The last thing I need is for deaths to increase because they faint on the machinery!"

Prudence shuddered. Accidents did occasionally happen, and it was hard to bear when a worker was killed. It often had resounding consequences for the whole family of the victim.

"If there is anything I can do, just let me know. Now that Mr. Huxley spends his time with Anne, I am able to help," Prudence said.

"I shall be speaking to Huxley. He has a sharp brain, and I think among the three of us we can sort something out quickly. I have already spoken to the foremen and told them of my intentions."

"Good. Hopefully, we can come up with something that will help."

The journey home was uneventful, and on arrival at the house, Prudence immediately went to check on Anne. She was awake and smiled to see her cousin enter her chamber.

"What? No Mr. Huxley?" Prudence asked in surprise.

"I asked him to leave the last time I needed to sleep. I made him promise he would go for a walk in the gardens. He has been with me for so much of each day, I am worried about him finding it tedious, spending so much time with me in a sick room," Anne admitted.

"I would be very surprised if he thought that. He is the man you are to marry. If he can't stand a few days of inactivity, it is a sad state of affairs."

There had been a long discussion when Fitzwilliam's letter had arrived saying that Lady Catherine had undergone a change of heart and would now approve a marriage between Anne and Mr. Huxley. Fitzwilliam had outlined his suggestion to his aunt about them not returning immediately to Rosings and Anne had been brought to tears by the fact she was going to marry the man she loved and spend time travelling.

Anne smiled at Prudence's words. "I know I shall be a drain on his patience."

"As he has known you these last ten years, I doubt that very much. Have confidence in yourself, Anne. You are lovely."

"You are very kind. I wish I could take you with us on our trip. Would you not like to see France and perhaps Italy, if I can persuade Mama to travel a little further?"

"I thank you for your invitation, but no. I doubt Lady Catherine could tolerate my tendency to impertinence for long periods of time. I will promise to come and visit you when you return to England."

"I shall keep you to your word."

"And who knows, you might have caught the travel bug and return to visit me here, but with less adventure, next time," Prudence teased.

"Definitely nicer inns and clean, warm sheets next time," Anne said, with a grimace.

"Yes. When one is running away from home, it is advisable to plan ahead first."

"Believe me, I have learned my lesson."

"Good."

*

The following morning Prudence entered the breakfast room to find Mr. Huxley seated alone.

"Has my father left for the mills already?" she asked in surprise.

"Yes. A while ago, apparently. I was wondering if you would mind being with Anne today whilst I travel to the mill? I've been thinking about the plans Mr. Bamber would like to implement, and in my chamber this morning, I wrote down some suggestions. I was hoping to go through them over breakfast, but he managed to avoid me," Mr. Huxley said with a smile.

"I am sure you must be his long-lost son for you do seem to be like two peas in a pod where business is concerned. He is going to miss you when you are gone," Prudence said. "Of course, I will remain with Anne. It would be my pleasure."

"Thank you. I shall check on her before I leave."

"I hope you are able to organise something sooner rather than later. I had not realised the situation was so bad. That is what comes of spending weeks removed from the real world."

Mr. Huxley smiled as he cut up a thick slice of ham. "I think Lady Catherine prefers not to have the outside world intrude as much as possible. Ever."

"She is going to have her equilibrium upset then whilst travelling abroad. Or, should I say you will have much to bear?"

"As employers go, she isn't too bad," Mr. Huxley admitted.

"Really? I doubt I could work for her."

"Oh, I don't know. You managed a few weeks without exploding."

Prudence laughed. "I did. I must have more forbearance than I give myself credit for. I admire you for being in her employ for ten years."

"I had bright spots in my day," Mr. Huxley said, a flush tinging his cheeks.

"Yes. You did, I suppose. You are both very lucky to have each other. I wish you all the happiness in the world."

"Thank you."

Chapter 21

A commotion downstairs brought Prudence out of Anne's chamber a few hours after breakfast. She could hear Mr. Huxley's voice in the hall, and he sounded agitated.

Quickly descending the stairs, she saw that the usually calm gentleman was flushed and a little wild eyed.

"Mr. Huxley, whatever is wrong? Are you ill?"

"Miss Bamber, please excuse my early return. I tried to reach the mills to see your father, but we just couldn't get the carriage through. I have never seen anything like it before in my life! There are people everywhere! It's like a swarm moving through the streets. No vehicles are moving. Not into the city anyway," Mr. Huxley said in a rush.

Prudence's heart started to pound but she kept her expression bland. "You poor thing. Why don't you go to Anne, and I shall have some tea sent to you? I am sure the crowds will disperse soon enough."

"But Mr. Bamber — "

"Papa will be safe enough behind the mill gates. No one will breach those," Prudence assured him.

"I did not like being forced to turn around, but I was putting the horses and coachman at risk," Mr. Huxley said. It was clear he was shaken and upset at what he had seen and felt that he had abandoned the man who had given him so much.

"Please. You took the right course of action. Go to Anne. She will be wondering what is amiss, because I left her chamber in a hurry when I heard your entrance. Do not worry about Papa or the mill."

Prudence waited until Mr. Huxley had disappeared up the stairs and was out of sight. She turned to the butler.

"Miss Prudence," he warned, knowing full well the direction her thoughts were headed.

Prudence smiled despite feeling desperate to reach her father. "I know the cut-throughs and the side streets. I shall travel on horseback."

"Mr. Bamber would flog me if I allowed you to leave the safety of the house to venture into goodness knows what," the butler said.

Shoulders sagging, Prudence sighed. "It isn't fair. You know I would not be able to leave the house in all conscience, although Papa would not dream of flogging anyone, a matter you are fully aware of. It is cruel to make me feel guilty at the possibility."

"He might," came the deadpan response.

"Pfft," Prudence responded. "If you could send refreshments up to Lady Anne's chamber, that would be appreciated. I will not disturb them. I think Mr. Huxley will only feel guilty if he sees me. I shall read in my chamber."

The butler narrowed his eyes at Prudence, but she smiled sweetly at him and retraced her steps upstairs.

When the loyal servant entered Anne's chamber with a tray laden with tea and delicacies, Prudence ran quietly back downstairs. Yes, she had gone to her chamber, but only to dress herself in her riding habit.

Veering away from the front door, she entered the dining room, thankful she had made it downstairs without being seen. She opened one of the full-length windows and stepped out to the side of the house. It reminded her of the time at Rosings when she had escaped from the library with Fitzwilliam. The thought made her smile. Closing the window, she hurried across the paving stones and headed around the back of the house to the stables.

"Saddle Scarlett for me please, John," she said to the stable-hand when she walked into the stable block.

"Scarlett, Miss Prudence?" came the surprised response.

"Yes." Prudence could not help a smile twitching her lips. Scarlett was the calmest of the whole stable; nothing seemed to worry her. She was far too docile to go cantering over the fields at a neck-or-nothing speed, but she was perfect to be ridden into an unknown situation with crowds of people. Prudence hoped so anyway.

"The coachman said it was very dangerous in the city, Miss Prudence," John said.

Prudence could have stamped her foot in frustration. The trouble with staff who had known you for years was that they tended to guess your actions. "I know. I need to find my father and get him to leave the city."

"Let me come with you."

"No! I will be quicker on my own. I shall go straight to the mill. I understand the carriage could not get through, but I'll be able to avoid the main streets. I am more than capable of fending for myself. A crowd of workers does not frighten me."

"You'd be safer with my escort. Your father would certainly agree."

"He would also curse me to the devil for inconveniencing you for no reason. The streets are full. The mill is in no danger. We shall return in Papa's carriage as soon as the crowds have gone."

"I'd be happier if I accompanied you."

"I am going on my own, John. Your escort is unnecessary. How many hundreds of times have I travelled it alone? I will be safe."

John did not look convinced, but he knew, one way or another, Prudence would find a way into the city. Better on horseback than walking, which he was sure she would try if he refused to saddle the horse.

Prudence waited impatiently until Scarlett was ready, and then using the mounting block, she settled herself in the saddle, and nodding her goodbye, turned the horse towards the gate.

"Come on, girl. We are to find Papa."

The closer Prudence got to the city centre, the more people she had to try to steer her way around. Most of the time she was ignored, but occasionally she would receive a curse. People were walking in the road as well as on the pavement, slowing anything down. She understood why the carriage had struggled to get through. She was finding it difficult enough.

Using some of the side streets as cut throughs, she had almost reached her father's largest mill before movement was severely restricted. She coaxed Scarlett on, feeling sorry for the beast who was now surrounded by people in a way she had never been before.

The crowd was tense rather than angry. A few people recognised Prudence and shouted comments to her. At one point one of the old foremen from her father's mill called up to her.

"Miss Bamber! You need to get away from here!" he shouted to her above the noise of the crowd.

"I need to get to the mill!" Prudence answered, but she was beginning to think she would never reach it. Afraid

202

of being unable to push through if she dismounted, she was grimly clinging to the reins and urging Scarlett forward.

The foreman pushed his way through the throng and reached her side. "Trying to get through this crowd is madness!" he scolded her.

"I agree! But I can't turn back now," she insisted. "Would you take care of my horse if I carried on by foot?"

"It's not safe," he said. "They are wanting someone's blood, and it could get serious very quickly. It's only going to take a spark, and it will turn nasty. Let me lead you to the mill. I need to get you away from here."

Taking hold of the reins, the foreman pushed and cursed his way through the crowd. Prudence had doubted that he would have more of an impact than she would on a horse, but he did. It probably had more to do with the fact that most people knew him and responded to his cursing.

Eventually, they reached Bamber Mill, and he stepped to the side. "Take some advice Miss Bamber. Don't leave the mill until the crowds have completely dispersed. It is not safe, and when we lose the light, goodness knows what will happen."

He rattled the gate, and the watchman came from his brick building at the side of the gate. He looked astonished to see Prudence but quickly unlocked the large iron structure and allowed Prudence and the horse entrance into the quiet mill yard.

Prudence turned to thank the foreman for his help, but he had already disappeared into the crowds. Feeling more unsettled than she ever had, she quickly dismounted.

"Please tell me my father is here and not at the other mill," she said.

"He's here, Miss Bamber. The looms are quiet though. Never known it like this 'afore."

"No. Nor I," Prudence admitted before taking Scarlett into the part of the yard in which the horses and her father's carriage were stored. She helped the coachman settle the horse and warned him they would not be leaving for some time. Securing Scarlett, Prudence gave her a pat and apologised for her mistreatment on the journey.

Walking into the mill, which was eerily quiet she took off her gloves and hat. Heading straight to the office, her footsteps echoed across the empty, still room. The looms were suspended mid-action, where they had ceased working when the power had ceased.

Mr. Bamber looked up in surprise when she opened the office door without knocking.

"Prudence, what the devil are you doing here?" he demanded upon realising who was coming into his office.

"Mr. Huxley had to turn back on his way in. He told me of the crowds and the strange behaviour of everyone. I had to come to you," Prudence said.

"And put yourself in goodness knows what danger?" The normally amiable gentleman was furious.

"I had to make sure you were safe."

"I was a lot better off when I knew you were secure in Stretford, well away from all this trouble!"

"I am sorry, but I would not have been able to rest."

"Prudence, I've no idea when this is going to pass over. We could be here all night."

"At least this way, I know you might be uncomfortable and hungry but not in any danger. My imagination would have kept me worrying if you had not returned. I am even more convinced that, for me at least, I made the right decision." Prudence sat on one of the wooden chairs. "Why has this escalated so quickly?"

"The workers and the jobless have decided to march to show their displeasure at the low wages, lack of jobs, and prices of goods. I do not understand the willingness for whole families to lose at least a days' pay when they are already struggling to feed themselves, but then I am not in their position," Mr. Bamber explained.

"It seems so unfocused an activity when I was travelling through the streets. Are they aiming for somewhere specific?"

"Any open spaces where speakers can make rallying speeches, I think. Some of the other mill owners have threatened that they won't have the workers back if they return to work tomorrow."

"And you?"

"If I see any trouble-makers causing problems or delays to the production lines, they will be dismissed, but so far I will accept a day strike. They want to make a point, and as long as there is no damage, there will be no harm done."

"It will cost you though."

"Aye, it will. It will not cripple us quite yet, so there's no need to worry."

Prudence smiled. "As you are the most astute businessman I know, I am not worried in the slightest."

"I am honoured. You are on first name terms with most of the mill owners in this town. You obviously know what talent there is out there."

"Which just shows how much faith I have in you."

A noise outside drew them both to the window, which overlooked the yard and the gates. They watched in silence for a few moments as the crowds continued to surge and occasionally the gates rattled in protest.

"If they get inside the yard, there will be mischief," Mr. Bamber said.

"Will the gates hold?"

"I hope so."

Prudence felt the first stirrings of unease. She had been so confident making her way in, arrogantly presuming that, as the daughter of a respected master, nothing untoward would happen to her. Doubts had started to crowd in on her when she had been outside until she was rescued by the foreman. Having felt safe in the familiar surroundings once inside the mill, hearing the uncertainty in her father's voice suddenly made her feel insecure in their position.

Gathering her courage, she turned and smiled at her father. "I shall make tea on your fire. Do you have anything to eat? If we are to stay here tonight I hope you have, or we shall be reduced to toasting one of your ledgers!"

"Fortunately for my paperwork, I always bring a parcel of food from home. One never knows when one will become peckish, and the shops around here probably make their bread with more brick dust than flour."

"It's a blessing that you come prepared." Prudence busied herself. The parcel her father handed her contained enough bread, ham, and cheese to split it for an early meal for them. She put some on one side. "I will take this to Mick at the gate and Fred in the stables. They must be equally as worried about what's going on and hungry too."

"It will take a lot to upset Mick," Mr. Bamber said. "Quite a few people have been shown off the premises by Mick, and they haven't dared to threaten him. He is very handy with his fists when needed."

"Good to know. Although I hope that won't be necessary."

The pair ate their repast, and then Prudence took portions out to the two workers still on the site. Fred was more than happy to remain with the horses.

"They are used to the noise of the mill. No crowds will disturb these beauties," he said, accepting the bread and cheese gratefully whilst answering Prudence's questions.

"Good. As soon as we can, we'll return to Stretford, but it will probably be dark by the time we leave."

"I will be ready in the shortest time. We will get home safe and sound. Don't worry, Miss Bamber."

"I have every faith in you," Prudence said, before leaving the stable and walking over to the gate.

The amount of people passing had not let up. She smiled grimly at Mick as he came out of his small office. "I didn't think there were so many people in Manchester," she admitted.

"I have been listening to them passing," Mick said. "I don't think they are all from around here, which isn't good."

"No loyalty?"

"No, Miss. There will be trouble 'afore the night's out," Mick warned.

Giving him the food, Prudence did not hang around near the gate. She found the situation unnerving. Hurrying back to her father's office, she wrapped her arms around her middle. The sooner they could return home, the better.

Chapter 22

Of all the days for a thick yellow fog to curl its way through the streets of Manchester, today was not the one for it to happen. Unfortunately, the weather failed to comply with what the populace would have liked it to do, and fog snaked its way down every road and alleyway, enfolding everyone on the streets in its thick choking smog.

Some of the strikers decided that they had had enough of an adventure and did not wish to struggle through the fog any longer, and they started to return home. Mick had reported that there seemed to be a surge of people travelling in the opposite direction, clearly seeking out their homes, in which there would be an escape from the dark, damp air.

Prudence had been worried that she had no longer been able to see the gate clearly, but Mick had sent Fred up to reassure them that there was the possibility of a ceasing of activity.

Fred returned to the stables, but then it seemed that there was a roar outside the mill gates and some sort of commotion. He joined Mick, and they both tried to peer through the mist to work out what was going on.

Some folk grabbed the gates and rattled the metal, begging to be allowed into the yard.

"Be off wi' thee!" Mick shouted. "T'mill's shut!"

"Let us in, or we'll be crushed!" more than one voice appealed.

"We're not daft. You will get up to no mischief here tonight. Be gone!"

The noise seemed to increase. Shouting, running, and shoving was taking place. More and more people were being pushed against the gate, and Mick looked in alarm at Fred. "Best get the master. I don't think they're funning. Looks like they're being pushed up against the gates," Mick said quietly.

Fred set-off at a run into the mill and up the stairs. Arriving breathless he repeated what Mick had said.

"What the devil is happening out there?" Mr. Bamber demanded. "Come on Fred. Let's go and have a look."

"I am coming with you," Prudence said, immediately standing.

"Oh, no you are not, Missy," Mr. Bamber said pausing mid-step. "You are going to promise me that you will remain here and lock the door behind me."

"But I—"

"No buts, Prudence. I do not know what is going on, and I am not letting you go headlong into a scrape. I accept you would have been more worried sitting at home, but in this instance you will listen to me and do as I say," Mr. Bamber said, all his usual mildness gone.

"Fine, but you must promise to return as soon as you can," Prudence acquiesced.

"No following me?"

"No. I promise. I shall lock the door the moment you leave the office." She would be troubled the whole time he was out of the mill building but knew she had to obey his wishes. It was not fair for him to be worried about her.

"Good."

Mr. Bamber left the office with Fred, and Prudence did as she promised. She stood at the window but could see hardly anything, the fog was so thick. When the footsteps of the two men had died away, she was left to listen to the ticking of the clock. Time was going to drag until her father returned.

Mick seemed relieved to see his master arrive at the mill gates. Mr. Bamber did not need to ask what was going on; he could see and hear enough to know there was a problem outside the mill.

Pleading voices begged him to let them into the yard.

"Open the gates," Mr. Bamber instructed Mick.

"Are you sure, sir?"

"Yes. Otherwise, people are going to get crushed. I have no idea what's going on, but I do know these people are in danger."

Mick reluctantly released the lock on the gates and had to step back quickly to get out of the way of the surge of people who stumbled into the now unrestricted space. Dozens of people filled the yard, with more following.

"What's happening?" Mr. Bamber asked one of the men he recognised.

"There's rioting started, sir. Some mischief makers from across the Pennines have come to stir up trouble," the man explained. "They have been charging at mills and causing all sorts of damage. The cavalry are driving them back, but that just means that we at the back were being pushed farther and farther back into smaller places. Thank you for opening the gates."

Mr. Bamber looked around. It would not be long before the mill yard would fill if people continued to pour in as they were still doing. "You need to return home."

"We can't turn everyone around," the man said. "There are some at the back still wanting to reach the fight at the front. It's madness."

"Damn it," Mr. Bamber muttered half to himself. He turned to Mick. "When the yard is full we close the gates again. I am not letting it overfill, and we just cause a crush in here instead of outside."

There was some shouting out of the gate, and a group of men rushed into the yard. "Up the workers!" they shouted, waving arms and batons in the air.

Starting to strike anything they could, a few others began to follow them. Mr. Bamber and Mick rushed at the original group but were thrown off in their attempts to stop any damage to the property in the yard.

A hard baton struck Mr. Bamber between his shoulders as he fought with one of the ring leaders. "I stopped you being crushed!" he gasped as the pain ripped across his back.

"You're making money while your workforce starves," the man in front of him snarled and brought the baton down on the side of his head.

Mr. Bamber fell to the ground.

*

Fitzwilliam charged along with his fellow cavalrymen. The order had been given to try to disperse the crowd without causing injury. It had been a vain hope.

Since his arrival at the barracks in which they were housed, he had been desperate to get a message to the

211

Bambers or to see Prudence. Unfortunately for him, his late arrival had meant that, as soon as he had been brought up to date with what was happening, he was sent out on duty.

That had been yesterday, but today things had changed.

He had been moving closer to Bamber Mills with the crowds and the cavalry. He had been told that most places were closed for the day, the workers going on strike, but he was uneasy as to whether Mr. Bamber was in the mill. He knew the man's work ethic and did not think he would have willingly taken a day off work.

When the fog descended it was as if the whole atmosphere of the people changed. During the afternoon it had been tense — a sort of uneasy stand-off between the uniformed horsemen and the workers, but they had continued on their way whilst the cavalry had just watched them.

Then the fog had started to swirl, and the mostly good-natured singing and some of the rallying speeches had taken on another tone completely. All of a sudden there were cries demanding action by the gathered mob and yelling, stirring a ripple of unrest and unease.

A small charge from the front of the crowd caused chaos, some people trying to escape, some to turn back, and others to push forward. All the time shouts were ringing out.

Then the clubs and chains came from underneath coats and out of pockets. That was the moment they had been instructed to try to disrupt what could easily turn into a major riot.

Fitzwilliam had surged forward, trying to cause confusion in the crowd and separate who they had seen as ringleaders. There was a mass of men and women, even some children, all intent on avoiding the snorting horses in their midst.

He had no idea how they found out, but one of the men called out that the mill gates further down the street had been breached. Fitzwilliam's stomach lurched at the news, and he urged his horse forward. He had to get to Bamber Mill to make sure all was well.

Kicking anyone out of the way who aimed a club in his direction, or using a baton of his own, he surged forward. He knew that many would be innocents caught up in an activity they would probably be regretting by now, so he was careful not to cause unnecessary injury. He was a just man, and although set against the ones who were armed, he could not just trample over the ones who were trying to reach safety.

It seemed like an eternity before the large opening to Bamber Mills loomed out of the fog. If a mill was awe-inspiring during a clear day, it was haunting encased by fog. Unfortunately, Fitzwilliam did not have time to appreciate the monster building engulfed in swirls of smoke. He was too intent on making sure Mr. Bamber was not present.

Seeing the gates open, Fitzwilliam cursed that this had to be the mill that was breached. People were still inside, but his entrance caused some to push their way through the opening and back onto the street. He could hear the smashing of glass and looked around wildly to see if there was anyone he recognised.

As he pushed forward, he noticed a crouched form and shouting out, he caused the man to move slightly.

"Dear God," Fitzwilliam uttered before flinging himself out of the saddle. He strode over to where Mick was crouched over Mr. Bamber's prone body. "Is he alive?" he asked.

"Yes, sir," Mick answered.

"Thank God for that! We need to get him inside. Is there no one else to help?"

"Fred is protecting the animals. All the rest of the workforce is off. Mr. Bamber was only stopping them being crushed against the gates, sir. He was helping them, and they started to cause damage," Mick babbled, clearly shaken by what he had seen and trying to protect his employer from swarming bodies who had shown they did not mind attacking a lone man.

Fitzwilliam looked at the building. He could not see clearly but he could hear the sound of windows being broken. He needed to get Mr. Bamber away, but there was something making him pause in lifting the injured man onto his horse.

The sound of shattering glass made Mick wince, and he looked at Fitzwilliam. "Sir. Miss Prudence is in the mill."

"What?" Fitzwilliam almost shouted at him.

"She's locked in the office," Mick said.

Feeling sick to his stomach, Fitzwilliam drew out his sword from the hilt on his belt. They had been given strict instructions. No swords out.

Damn that to the devil.

The woman he loved was in a building that was being ransacked.

He set off at a run.

*

Prudence could not see the gates, but she saw the number of people surging into the yard. She stepped back away from the window, for some reason not wishing to be

214

seen. Watching at a discreet distance, she became more concerned as the noise increased.

Starting to pace the office from one side to the other, she jumped in alarm at the first sound of smashing glass. The voices had risen shortly beforehand, and she knew without doubt that the situation had changed.

Choking back a sob of fear, not for herself, but that her father and two of his loyal workers were amongst whatever was going on, she started to search her father's drawers.

Surprised but pleased, she found a gun tucked away in the bottom drawer of his desk. With shaking hands she managed to load the gun and prime it, before looking out the window once more.

Not able to see enough of what was happening, she took up a place behind her father's chair and waited.

Time seemed to slow down, but moment after moment seemed to bring the noise of the destruction ever closer. Voices rose and cried out, but nothing was clear to her. She had never felt so out of control of events in her life, and she just hoped that no one would think of starting a fire.

If they did, all hope would be lost, for she would never get out of the building alive. Yet, she knew that for the present, being behind a locked door was safer than trying to make her escape.

Hearing footsteps running outside the office, she stood straighter and pointed the gun at the door. Wiping a bead of sweat from her forehead before putting her other hand on the gun to steady it, she silently cursed herself for her feebleness. She was descended from tough, hard-working stock. She would not allow fear to overtake her.

Standing still, she watched the door.

The rattle of the doorknob made her swallow.

"Prudence, are you inside?" Fitzwilliam shouted from beyond the door.

"Fitzwilliam!" Prudence cried, hardly able to believe whose voice was calling to her.

"Yes! It is I! Open the door!" Fitzwilliam demanded.

Prudence put the gun onto the desk and ran to the door. Flinging the wooden structure open, she did not wait for Fitzwilliam to enter the room but fell into his arms.

Fitzwilliam staggered a little at the force with which she flung herself at him, but he wrapped one arm around her, keeping his sword out of the way with his other. Kissing her hair, he squeezed her tightly.

"I thought they might have reached you. I feared you'd been discovered," he said into her hair. "I wanted to kill everyone in that yard to get to you."

Prudence laughed with a sob in her voice. "I wanted to leave but I'd promised Papa. Have you seen him?" Keeping her arms around his neck she pulled back a little to look him in the eye.

"He's downstairs. He has been hurt, but he is alive," Fitzwilliam said. There was no point in hiding the truth from her, having no idea how Mr. Bamber was.

"No! I must go to him!" Prudence said, rushing into the office and grabbing the gun.

"And what do you think you are going to do with that?" Fitzwilliam could not stop the twinkle of amusement in his eyes.

"It is in case anyone gets in our way," Prudence answered.

"Give it to me. I think I will feel safer knowing my hands are shaking a little less than yours."

"Beast." Prudence handed Fitzwilliam the gun. Her hands were indeed still shaking, and she would more than likely have shot herself in the foot than injured anyone else, but it did not lessen the urge to see her father.

"Keep behind me," Fitzwilliam instructed as they started to move across the loom floor.

"Is there much destruction?" Prudence asked as they walked.

"I don't know. I think a lot of windows have been broken, but it does not matter. Material things can be replaced. You and your father are all that matter to me."

His words warmed her insides, which had been chilled throughout her ordeal. She positioned herself so he shielded her, her hand on his shoulder so he knew she was there. They walked outside in their odd convoy, Fitzwilliam pushing away anyone who dared to come near him. Having his sword in one hand and a pistol in the other tended to put most people off. They veered around him.

As he approached the gate, he breathed a relieved sigh that there were two more cavalry officers in the gate area of the mill. He called to them, and they looked in surprise at him.

"Preparing for a real battle?" one of the men asked when seeing how he was armed.

"The mill owner has been injured, and his daughter was trapped in the mill," Fitzwilliam explained, tucking the pistol into his belt.

"Good God."

"Exactly. We need this area cleared and the gates secured. Mr. Bamber only opened the gates because people were being crushed. He's been attacked for being considerate. I would like to flog everyone in this damned yard," Fitzwilliam said.

"You get him home. We will sort this out," the second officer said. The grim line in which his lips were

217

compressed made Fitzwilliam think that a few of the strikers would have sore heads by morning.

"I should stay," Prudence said quietly.

"No. They have said they will take over, and they will. The important thing is to get you both home."

Prudence crouched near her father when they reached him. He was conscious, which was a huge relief to Fitzwilliam. He had feared the worst but hadn't wished to frighten Prudence.

Mr. Bamber was groggy and in pain, but he was helped into his carriage, which was brought through the crowds, escorted by the two baton-wielding cavalry men.

"There you go, sir! Safe journey home. Don't worry about a thing! All will be right and tight here!"

Not seeming to be aware of what was going on around him, Mr. Bamber was helped into the carriage by Mick and Fitzwilliam. Fred was atop the vehicle, bracing himself for what would be a perilous journey, however necessary.

Prudence climbed in behind her father and forced him to lie down, putting his head on her knee.

"If there is any change in him, let me know. I will be riding by your side the whole way home," Fitzwilliam said before closing the door on them. Turning to Mick he nodded his head. "Thank you for what you've done this evening in protecting Mr. Bamber. You probably saved him from being trampled. You will not be left alone until the site is perfectly secure and everyone has been dispersed."

"Thank you, sir. Tell Mr. Bamber not to worry. I shall remain here all night," Mick said.

"Good man." Fitzwilliam climbed onto his horse and indicated to Fred to drive the carriage. He had no idea how long it was going to take them to get home, but he would

218

have no compunction about trampling over anyone who tried to maliciously stop them.

Chapter 23

The house was thrown into activity the moment the carriage came to a halt outside the door. Prudence suspected there had been a watch looking out for them.

Many hands helped Mr. Bamber to his chamber, and his valet undressed him and settled him in his bed before the doctor arrived.

After checking him over and administering some laudanum and waiting until it took effect, he turned to Prudence who had been present in her father's chamber since the doctor arrived.

"I am confident there will be no permanent injury or effects. He has had a knock, and although it stunned him for a while and he will have a lump for days, I am sure he will be his usual self in a day or two. Make him rest at least for a day and then he can start to move around his chamber. I suggest a week before he returns to work. Just to be on the safe side."

"Oh, dear. He has never had so much time away from the mill," Prudence said.

"Tell him I insist," the doctor said with a smile.

"That might not be enough."

"It would be wise to allow the swelling to go down. He could cause further problems if he ignores my advice."

"I will ensure he abides by it," Prudence assured him, showing him out the door.

When the doctor left, she went into the drawing room and was glad to see Fitzwilliam waiting there.

"How is he?" Fitzwilliam asked, standing as Prudence entered the room.

"He should be fine if he takes the next week off and rests."

Fitzwilliam laughed. "Good luck with that."

"Exactly! How the devil am I going to persuade him to do that?"

"Language, Prudence! What would Aunt Catherine say?"

"She would think me the lost cause I am."

"How are you? Did you get the doctor to check you over as well?"

"No. I am perfectly well. It just keeps replaying like some sort of waking nightmare. What if you had not arrived when you did? What if father had received further injuries?"

Fitzwilliam crossed the space between them and enfolded her in his arms. She rested her head on his shoulder with relief. "The imagined outcomes will pass," he said, gently rubbing her back.

"I could have lost him," Prudence choked out. "I would have been alone."

Fitzwilliam pulled away from her slightly. "You didn't lose him, and even if you had, you would not have been alone. I am here. I will always be here."

"Oh, Fitzwilliam! Have I been foolish in my criticism of you? Was I being unfair?" Prudence asked, feeling as if she were no longer sure of anything.

"I let you down. I understand that," Fitzwilliam said gently. "I am going to make sure I spend every day convincing you that I am worth another chance. Because I am. We are."

"It would be so easy to fall back to how we were," Prudence said. "All I want is to remain within your arms, but there are too many hurdles to overcome."

"Shhh, you aren't thinking straight after what has happened today. Just take comfort. Do not make decisions about your future just yet. There is lots of time." Holding her close once more, he continued to rub her back gently until the tension started to ease from her shoulders. When she felt completely relaxed, he once more moved away slightly. When she grumbled at his actions, he smiled. "I need to return to Manchester."

"Oh, no! Don't go! You will be in danger again," Prudence said. The misty look had disappeared from her expression, which was now all concern at his words.

"I have to go, but I promise I shall be safe. Might I visit first thing in the morning?"

"Of course. Please be careful."

"I will." Taking her face in his hands, he kissed her lips gently. "I love you, Prudence. Just for being you. Never forget that."

*

Prudence awoke late in the morning. She had fallen asleep hours after going to bed, and she had a throbbing headache pounding at her temple, making her wince as she was helped to dress. Checking on her father, she was told he had been awake, but although he had eaten a little, he'd fallen asleep soon afterwards.

She entered the breakfast room to find Mr. Huxley and Fitzwilliam waiting for her. She smiled wanly. "Good morning to you both," she said.

"Come. Sit down. You look fit to drop," Fitzwilliam said. "Sleep elude you, did it? I thought it might." Busying himself in getting her a drink and some foodstuffs, he chatted cheerfully. "The mob had all but dispersed by the time I returned. There have been a number of arrests among miscreants, who will be appearing before the magistrates this morning."

"I need to go to the mill," Prudence said.

"About that," Fitzwilliam said bringing a plate to her and taking the seat next to her.

"Why am I suddenly worried?"

"Wretch! Have you no faith in us?"

Prudence took a sip of her tea and looked at the two indignant expressions staring at her. She laughed. "Fine. I have every faith in your abilities! What have you been concocting between the pair of you?"

"You father needs to rest. Mr. Huxley has a little experience about the mill's workings day-to-day, and although I have none, I am very interested in learning. We propose that we spend the next week working in the mill in place of your father. Admittedly, we might need to seek his counsel, but we thought he might enjoy being able to order us about from his chamber," Fitzwilliam explained.

"What about your other duties?" Prudence asked.

"I have decided to resign my commission," Fitzwilliam admitted. The look on Prudence's face made him laugh. "I wasn't going to tell you quite so soon, but you are a meddling woman who needs to know everything!"

"And you call me the wretch!" Prudence said.

"I shall go and check on Anne," Mr. Huxley said, discreetly removing himself from the room and the conversation that was going to take place.

"I like him," Fitzwilliam admitted.

"Oh, how things can change in a few weeks!" Prudence laughed.

"Yes, they can. Talking of which, I shall be speaking to your father and asking him if I would be allowed to pay my addresses to his beautiful daughter. I shall tell him that, although I can offer her little with regards to finances, I would like to be taken on as some sort of apprentice and learn the workings of the mill. Hopefully, in time to work side-by-side with him, and then one far off day, with my wife."

"Oh. I see."

"That isn't an encouraging response."

"No. But it would mean you work in trade and live in the north!" Prudence exclaimed.

Laughing Fitzwilliam lifted one of her hands and kissed her fingers. "I do not care where I live if it means I can eventually marry you. As for being in trade, I have long since known that I would have to leave the cavalry if I were to have a family. I had no idea what I was going to do, but when I went to the mill, it was almost as if I had arrived home. It felt so right to be there, so invigorating. Something I knew, without understanding the finer details, that I would be perfectly at home with."

Prudence looked at him as if considering his words and then a smile lifted her lips. "You would even be able to cope with the mill girls?"

"Ah, now that is one area in which I might struggle, but hopefully I would have my fearsome wife at my side."

"You really are a coward aren't you?"

"Most definitely. Now isn't it time you kissed me and said that you thought my plan was a good one?"

"I should curse you to the devil."

"Kissing is a far nicer occupation."

"I suppose it is."
"Then kiss me, Prudence, today and every day."
And she did just that.

Epilogue

Lady Anne De Bourgh and Mr. Huxley were married by special licence as soon as Anne was able to venture downstairs every day for a week. The married couple remained with the Bamber's for another month before it was decided that Anne was well enough to start their journey in slow, careful stages.

Lady Catherine and Mrs. Jenkinson travelled to meet them, having decided that they would not travel to Manchester for the wedding. Anne got to visit France, Spain, and Italy, only returning to Rosings two years after she had left.

As most people were curious to see the far stronger, happier, more outgoing Anne, the gossip about the start of her marriage was forgotten. After spending a few years at home, the couple departed once more for the continent, claiming that the warmer weather was far more beneficial to Anne's constitution. Some wondered if it were the distance from her mother that helped more than the weather, but none would openly say it. Anne did not have children but lived a long and happy life in Italy.

Colonel Fitzwilliam resigned his commission and joined the Bamber Mills. His father-in-law was delighted that the man who loved Prudence was willing and able when it came to mill business. Having been a very often overlooked second son, Fitzwilliam was to shine in the business arena.

His personality and intelligence were a perfect mix in negotiations, and it wasn't long before he was the one making the deals to benefit the two mills. This was especially important when cheaper imports started to flood the market, and the cotton industry began to struggle.

He eventually married the love of his life in a grand ceremony in Manchester Cathedral — only the best for Mr. Bamber's daughter. They had their own house built very close to Mr. Bamber, close enough that the grounds butted up against each other. It made visits to the well-loved grandfather all the easier when the six children came along.

Prudence never doubted that Fitzwilliam loved her for herself and not her fortune. Others, like Selina Beauchamp, might think so, but it didn't worry Prudence that there might be speculation. As she had fallen in love with Fitzwilliam very early in their acquaintance, she believed him when he professed the same. His actions were always those of a besotted fool, which she of course regularly pointed out to him, at which point he would kiss her into squeals and laughter.

They were a well-respected, happy couple, liked by those they came into contact with.

The Darcy family travelled to Stretford, and Fitzwilliam proudly showed Darcy around the mills. He timed it perfectly so the mill girls would be in the yard as they crossed it and was not disappointed at Darcy's discomfort at the raucous comments aimed at them. It kept Fitzwilliam laughing for days.

Prudence and Elizabeth were immediately drawn to each other. Similar in personality, they found amusement in the same situations and were both quick-witted and intelligent. Darcy and Fitzwilliam would often escape to the billiard room if the teasing attention of both women at the same time focused in their direction.

Darcy had cleared the air between himself and Prudence before her marriage to Fitzwilliam. He thought highly of his cousin and did not wish there to be any contention between the families, especially as they lived so close to each other.

Fitzwilliam's immediate family had been astounded at his change of career, but once they had seen him chatter on about the mill and all it entailed, they realised he had found his place in the world. Prudence was welcomed into the family, as was Mr. Bamber. They were the most relaxed branch of the family, and although Prudence had worried that her reception would be like the one she received with Lady Catherine, there was no formality or disdain, just a warm, genuine welcome.

The pair would never spend much time in London. Prudence never felt comfortable there, and Fitzwilliam did not like being so far away from the mills. He would be teased that he was turning into Mr. Bamber, at which he would defend his father-in-law completely.

Prudence and Fitzwilliam had found love despite prejudice and secrets. Their house was to be filled with laughter, and although Prudence had not had the connection with her Aunt Catherine that she'd wished to have in order to feel closer to the mother she missed so much, Fitzwilliam's mother and her new cousins more than made up for the fact that Lady Catherine would never truly welcome her into the family.

Prudence was happy and loved. Nothing else mattered.

About this book.

I have always wanted Colonel Fitzwilliam to have his happy ever after. Which is why I jumped at the chance of being part of the 'Love After All' Tragic Heroes in Classic Literature group. It was my opportunity to find him his true love.

There was definitely a flirtation between himself and Elizabeth, but he was clear in telling her that he needed to marry for money. Although I understand why he did it, I always thought it was a little arrogant of him. The situation always struck me when the story describes the exchange between Darcy and Elizabeth when Darcy seems to be suggesting that on her next visit to the area she shall be staying at Rosings. She presumes he means through a connection with Colonel Fitzwilliam and wait for it — she's disappointed! Proving (in my eyes anyway) that the thought of being married to Colonel Fitzwilliam wasn't something she wanted. Even then, Elizabeth was drawn to Darcy; she just wasn't recognising her feelings for what they were, and well, Darcy wasn't helping, really, was he? That first proposal! Oh, my word!

Jane Austen also describes Fitzwilliam as not handsome, but with a good personality. Damned by faint praise! If he needed to marry for money, I have often thought that he would have struggled to find a suitable woman within the *ton* circles. So, I had to bring in an outsider who would see how special he was.

As the tradesmen and particularly mill owners were extremely rich and I have a streak of mischief in me when pairing up opposites, it was inevitable that Fitzwilliam was going to marry outside of his social circle.

The country was going through difficulties after the Napoleonic Wars, and there was a lot of unemployment and beggars around who had come back from war on land or at sea and whose services were no longer required. A failure in harvests, the influx of foreign goods, the increased prices of food, and the restrictions of the Corn Laws meant there were riots and strikes across Britain from 1816.

If you look at Manchester and riots, the one in 1819 at Peterloo is obviously the one that is prominent in literature. I didn't want to tie this story into that. The timing didn't feel right, and I didn't want Fitzwilliam to be on the wrong side, so I kept my story as close to the 1813 date of Pride and Prejudice as I could, bearing in mind that Fitzwilliam would have been serving in the Napoleonic Wars himself, so I was happy to pick up his story after the wars had ended.

I hope you have enjoyed my take on Fitzwilliam's journey to his well-deserved happy ever after. As an author of Regency Romances, it has been both daunting and enjoyable to write this book and include some of the finest literary characters ever written.

Thank you for reading.

Audrey

About the Author

I have had the fortune to live a dream. I've always wanted to write, but life got in the way as it so often does until a few years ago. Then a change in circumstance enabled me to do what I loved: sit down to write. Now writing has taken over my life, holidays being based around research, so much so that no matter where we go, my long-suffering husband says, 'And what connection to the Regency period has this building/town/garden got?'

That dream became a little more surreal when in 2018, I became an Amazon StorytellerUK Finalist with Lord Livesey's Bluestocking. A Regency Romance in the top five of an all-genre competition! It was a truly wonderful experience, I didn't expect to win, but I had a ball at the awards ceremony.

I do appreciate it when readers get in touch, especially if they love the characters as much as I do. Those first few weeks after release is a trying time; I desperately want everyone to love my characters that take months and months of work to bring to life.

If you enjoy the books please would you take the time to write a review on Amazon? Reviews are vital for an author who is just starting out, although I admit to bad ones being crushing. Selfishly I want readers to love my stories!

I can be contacted for any comments you may have, via my website:

www.audreyharrison.co.uk

or

www.facebook.com/AudreyHarrisonAuthor

Please sign-up for email/newsletter – only sent out when there is something to say!

www.audreyharrison.co.uk

You'll receive a free copy of The Unwilling Earl in mobi format for signing-up as a thank you!

Novels by Audrey Harrison

Regency Romances – newest release first

Lady Edith's Lonely Heart – The Lonely Hearts Series – book 1

https://www.amazon.com/dp/B0852RMGJJ

https://www.amazon.co.uk/dp/B0852RMGJJ

Miss King's Rescue – The Lonely Hearts Series – book 2

https://www.amazon.com/dp/B08778RJQP

https://www.amazon.co.uk/dp/B08778RJQP

Captain Jones's Temptation – The Lonely Hearts Series – book 3

https://www.amazon.com/dp/B08775663R

https://www.amazon.co.uk/dp/B08775663R

The Lonely Lord

https://www.amazon.com/dp/B07S1X5NBZ

https://www.amazon.co.uk/dp/B07S1X5NBZ

The Drummond Series:-

Lady Lou the Highwayman – Drummond series Book 1

https://www.amazon.com/dp/B07NDX3HV2

https://www.amazon.co.uk/dp/B07NDX3HV2

Saving Captain Drummond – Drummond Series Book 2

https://www.amazon.com/dp/B07NFBRZFG

https://www.amazon.co.uk/dp/B07NFBRZFG

Lord Livesey's Bluestocking (Amazon Storyteller Finalist 2018)

https://www.amazon.com/dp/B07D3T6L93
https://www.amazon.co.uk/dp/B07D3T6L93

Return to the Regency – A Regency Time-travel novel

https://www.amazon.com/dp/B078C87HVX
https://www.amazon.co.uk/dp/B078C87HVX

My Foundlings:-

The Foundling Duke – The Foundlings Book 1

https://www.amazon.com/dp/B071KTT9CD
https://www.amazon.co.uk/dp/B071KTT9CD

The Foundling Lady – The Foundlings Book 2

https://www.amazon.com/dp/B072L2D7PF
https://www.amazon.co.uk/dp/B072L2D7PF

Book bundle – **The Foundlings**

https://www.amazon.com/dp/B07Q6YLND4
https://www.amazon.co.uk/dp/B07Q6YLND4

Mr Bailey's Lady

https://www.amazon.com/dp/B01NACMFVJ
https://www.amazon.co.uk/dp/B01NACMFVJ

The Spy Series:-

My Lord the Spy

https://www.amazon.com/dp/B01F11ZRM8
https://www.amazon.co.uk/dp/B01F11ZRM8

My Earl the Spy

https://www.amazon.com/dp/B01F12NG8E
https://www.amazon.co.uk/dp/B01F12NG8E

Book bundle – **The Spying Lords**

https://www.amazon.com/dp/B07RV3JQFP
https://www.amazon.co.uk/dp/B07RV3JQFP

The Captain's Wallflower

https://www.amazon.com/dp/B018PDBGLK

https://www.amazon.co.uk/dp/B018PDBGLK

The Four Sisters' Series:-

Rosalind – Book 1
https://www.amazon.com/dp/B00WWTXSA6
https://www.amazon.co.uk/dp/B00WWTXSA6

Annabelle – Book 2
https://www.amazon.com/dp/B00WWTXRWA
https://www.amazon.co.uk/dp/B00WWTXRWA

Grace – Book 3
https://www.amazon.com/dp/B00WWUBEWO
https://www.amazon.co.uk/dp/B00WWUBEWO

Eleanor – Book 4
https://www.amazon.com/dp/B00WWUBF1E
https://www.amazon.co.uk/dp/B00WWUBF1E

Book Bundle – **The Four Sisters**
https://www.amazon.com/dp/B01416W0C4
https://www.amazon.co.uk/dp/B01416W0C4

The Inconvenient Trilogy:-
The Inconvenient Ward – Book 1
https://www.amazon.com/dp/B00KCJUJFA
https://www.amazon.co.uk/dp/B00KCJUJFA

The Inconvenient Wife – Book 2
https://www.amazon.com/dp/B00KCJVQU2
https://www.amazon.co.uk/dp/B00KCJVQU2

The Inconvenient Companion – Book 3
https://www.amazon.com/dp/B00KCK87T4
https://www.amazon.co.uk/dp/B00KCK87T4

Book bundle – **An Inconvenient Trilogy**
https://www.amazon.com/dp/B00PHQIZ18
https://www.amazon.co.uk/dp/B00PHQIZ18

The Complicated Earl
https://www.amazon.com/dp/B00BCN90DC
https://www.amazon.co.uk/dp/B00BCN90DC
The Unwilling Earl (Novella)
https://www.amazon.com/dp/B00BCNE2HG
https://www.amazon.co.uk/dp/B00BCNE2HG

Other Eras
A Very Modern Lord
Years Apart

Printed in Great Britain
by Amazon